COLT AND CASSY

By

C. DEANNE ROWE

COLT AND CASSY
by C. Deanne Rowe

Published by Citrine Group, L.L.C.
Des Moines, IA

Cover Creation by Rebecca K. Sterling, Sterling Design Studios

First Printing: July 2020

ISBN-10: 978-1-946122-34-6
ISBN-13/EAN-13: 978-1-946122-34-6

Printed in the United States of America

DEDICATION

This book is dedicated to all the mommas who let their babies grow up to be cowboys...Thank you!

CHAPTER ONE

"Cowboy Butts Drive Me Nuts" Cassy read off the license plate frame she was holding up. "Where in the world?"

"Laura found it. Don't you love it?" Nancy clapped her hands together.

"I do love it." Cassy held it closer for inspection. "What am I supposed to do with this?"

"It's goes on the back of the truck you'll be driving around the farm." Laura laughed. "It might not hurt if you drove it around town every now and then. Who knows what you might pick up."

"Hah, very funny you guys. I'm going to put in on my SUV until I get to the farm." Cassy placed the gift back in the box. Besides, I'm not moving back to Oklahoma to pick up a cowboy. Although it might be nice to meet a few good-looking men while I'm there." She picked up her beer and held it up above the center of the table. "Here's to all good-looking cowboys."

"Here, here." Nancy joined Cassy holding up her beer.

"Same for me." Laura joined the two friends in a toast as all three clinked their glasses together then took a drink.

"I really hate to see you leave Cassy," Laura's smile turned into a pout.

"Me too. It's just not the same around the office without you." Nancy agreed.

"I'm going to miss you guys too, but fate has played its cards for me and it's Oklahoma here I come." Cassy paused for a moment. "I wasn't sure what to do when Grandpa got sick, but now I'm no longer employed by McGregor Oil, it's a good time for me to spend some time with him on the family farm."

"I can't believe you want to be a farmer," Nancy replied. "It doesn't fit for me."

"Why? I was practically raised on the family farm. My father couldn't leave fast enough when he got old enough and since he died five years ago that leaves me, if we want to keep the family farm up and running. Grandpa is in no shape." Cassy explained.

"I know, but you in your jeans, cowboy boots and hat riding a horse along the fence to make sure the cattle can't get out or driving the Caterpillar plowing or planting the fields. I just can't see you doing that," Laura replied.

"I guess you'll have to visit then, both of you. There's plenty of room and I'll take you for a ride in the truck. We'll see what kind of cowboys this license plate holder attracts." Cassy picked up her present and held it in the air.

"It's a deal." Both Laura and Nancy nodded their heads in agreement.

CHAPTER TWO

Cassy let herself in the older brick ranch house which seemed to be unoccupied. She looked around as she made her way to the spare bedroom down the hallway.

"Grandpa. I'm here."

Laying her luggage down on the bed, she wiped the beads of sweat that appeared on her forehead. The room looked the same as when she stayed with her grandparents over summer vacations. The double bed was covered with a quilt her grandmother had made. The curtains were pink checked which was her favorite color when she was little. There was the white dresser her grandfather had bought at a yard sale. He repaired one of the legs and she helped him paint it and place it lovely against the wall in her room. Such good memories.

The house was warm just like she remembered. It must be ninety degrees outside and yet the windows were wide open with a nice cool breeze blowing through.

"Grandpa must still be trying to save on the power bill." Cassy remembered him telling her that was the reason the windows were open instead of the air conditioning on.

She knew her grandparents never liked be shut up in the house. They wanted to feel part of nature and that meant outside air.

"I guess I'm going to have to adjust." She opened her suitcase and pulled out a pair of shorts and a light weight blouse to change into. Walking into the bathroom, Cassy ran cold water over her face and pulled her long brown hair up in a clip she found in her purse. "Much better."

"Cassandra Conner. Come give you old grandpa a hug."

Cassy walked back into the bedroom to see her grandfather, James Conner, in his wheelchair waiting in the doorway. She was surprised by the wheelchair. Last time she had seen him, he was using a cane.

"Grandpa." Cassy rushed toward him to give him a hug. "I was just coming to your room to find you. You look really good. You're up and around and you have lots of color in your cheeks." She patted his cheeks which made him smile. "When did you start using a wheelchair?"

"I started using it around the house to save my strength. I still use my cane when I'm out and about, but the wheelchair helps me save my strength for those times."

"That makes sense, but I hope you're still doing your exercises everyday like the doctors suggested."

"I do. You'll see that while you're here. Let's change the subject because I'm having a good day so I thought I would take advantage of it. Come with me to the kitchen and let's get a cold drink. I want to catch up and hear all about your trip. It's been so long."

"That sounds good." Cassy took the handles of his wheelchair and they headed to the kitchen. "What would you like? Some iced tea, some juice or maybe some milk and cookies."

"I vote for milk and cookies. Those darn nurses try to keep me on a strict diet because of this stupid diabetes." James shook his head.

"Well, then milk and cookies it'll be. I'm sure there's something in here we can snack on." Cassy searched through the sparsely filled pantry and found a stash of sugar free cookies. She poured each of them a glass of milk and put a few cookies on a plate and carried them to the table.

"Here we go. Enjoy."

"So, tell me about your trip, Cassandra."

Cassy took a seat at the kitchen table as she watched her grandfather take a bite of cookie and a drink of milk.

"Not much to tell Grandpa. It was long and tiring."

"Well, I'm glad you're here. I've really missed seeing you."

"I'm sorry I haven't visited more often, but work was crazy this past year. It seemed there was always some project to do. That was when I was under the impression I was a valued employee of the company and my killing myself with work was actually going to get me ahead." Cassy paused for a minute. "I guess they proved me wrong."

"There's one thing I want you to promise me Cassandra."

She could see the concern on his face as he reached for her hand. "What's that Grandpa?"

"I know you're coming back to help because of my health, but I don't want you to make this farm your first priority. There's so much more out there for you. You're a young woman and you have your entire life ahead of you. Your grandmother lived and breathed this farm and it killed her."

Cassy noticed the creases in his face deepen.

"This farm and me. We worked her to death. It's a hard life Cassandra."

"I know you think that Grandpa, but you know what, Grandmother wouldn't have wanted any other life. She loved you and this farm. This was where she wanted to be and she was happy. She always told me her life was complete. But I promise you I'll let you know if the farm gets to be too much. I'm not having my stuff moved out here until I'm sure I'm staying. How about that?" Cassy patted his hand.

"Sounds good to me. I'll hold you to it. Cassandra. You're a bright young lady. There'll always be something out there for you to do. There'll be other career paths for you to prove you're a valuable asset. Heck, I've known that since you were a little girl."

"You had to love me grandpa. I'm your granddaughter. But thanks for trying to make me feel better. Let's change the subject. So now, you tell me what's going on with the farm. What am I getting myself into?"

Cassy picked up the empty plate and took the milk from the refrigerator. She carefully poured them some more milk and placed a few more cookies on the plate.

"Well, we added a few more head of cattle, started charging for stud fees and selling semen from our prize bulls, planted a few more acres of wheat and soy beans. I believe we actually turned a profit this year."

Cassy noticed her grandfather's shoulder pull back with pride.

"How's your help working out? You must have some good people and they must be doing all right for you to show a profit."

"I only have one farmhand. When we are done here, we'll go out and meet Colt. He's the reason the farm's doing so well. He's a hard worker. I think you two will get along great."

"Let me clean up here then we'll go." Cassy picked up the plate and glasses, rinsed them off in the sink.

"Okay, let's go. Where's your cane?" Cassy started wheeling her grandfather towards the door when a muscular, tan, and tight-jeaned cowboy walked straight out of her dreams and through the kitchen door. He took off his cowboy hat and ran his hands through his thick coal black hair.

"Mr. Conner. I hope I'm not interrupting." His voice was deep and almost as sexy as he was.

"Not at all Colt. Come on in. We were just headed out the meet you." James motioned for Colt to come closer.

"You were?" Colt looked a little confused.

"Cassandra, this is Colt Matthews. I was just telling you about him. Colt, this is my granddaughter Cassandra Conner. I guess we're not gonna need my cane now."

Cassy watched as Colt walked towards her. She wished she had taken more time picking out something to wear now and maybe freshened up her makeup instead of just running cold water over her face. Had she known she was going to be meeting someone as handsome as Colt Matthews, she would have.

"It's nice to meet you, Ms. Conner." Colt extended his hand.

Cassy shook his hand noticing how hers seemed to disappear in his. His grip was firm and his skin calloused.

"Please, Colt, call me Cassy."

"Cassy. That's a nice name."

A smile crossed his face which seemed to light up his entire expression. He had one corner with turned up a little crooked giving him that bad boy look. Cassy was sure his mother had problems telling what he was up to when he was growing up.

"Thanks." She could feel her skin begin to blush. It was like she was back in high school.

"I just came in to tell you, Mr. Conner, I finished repairing the fence on the North end."

Colt may have taken his eyes off Cassy, but hers were firmly fixed on him.

"Good job. If you hadn't noticed the break in the fencing, we might've lost some of the cattle." James patted him on the leg. "Good job, Colt."

"I took a head count and everybody's accounted for. I'm going to go into town and get some supplies and grab some lunch. Did you make your list?" Colt asked.

"Yes, I did. It's over there on the counter. Let me get you some money."

Cassy watched her Grandfather grab the wheels of his chair and began to turn around.

"I'll get it, Grandpa. Show me where you keep your money and I'll be right back.

"I'll grab it. You stay here and keep Colt company." James Conner wheeled himself into the next room out of sight.

"Can I get you something to drink? It's horribly hot outside." Cassy fanned herself with her hand and tried break the silence in the room. There was something about Colt which pulled her to him. Cassy always had people radar, her father called it. Her radar was going off all over the place while she was in the room with Colt. She wasn't sure yet if it was good or bad.

"Sure. How about a glass of cold water?" Colt smiled.

"Sure." She grabbed the pitcher of cold water her grandfather always kept in the refrigerator and poured him a glass.

Cassy watched Colt take a drink. His skin was nice and tan with a little speckle of whiskers growing in. He wasn't bad looking at all for an Oklahoma cowboy.

"So, what brought you back to your grandpa's farm Cassy?"

"I was laid off my job in Texas. I thought I would take a little time and see if I could help Grandpa since he is alone here."

"Sorry to hear about your job. I'm sure your grandpa loves having you visit though."

She watched Colt take another drink of his water.

"I'm also sure he told you the farm was running smoothly. He wouldn't need your help there."

"Losing my job wasn't easy to accept at first, but I'm getting used to it. I'm sure you're doing a great job on the farm, Colt. I'm not here to take your job. I'm just here to help Grandpa."

Cassy could feel herself becoming frustrated. Didn't he know if something happened to her grandfather, she would be his boss? She was beginning to feel she was right back at McGregor Oil fighting for her position in a male dominated environment. The last thing she wanted to do right after arriving was relive those feelings.

"I could tell when I drove up everything looks great. But being here also gives me time to spend with Grandpa and make sure he's taking good care of himself." Cassy picked at the piece of lint on the tablecloth.

"Your grandfather's a tough old bird. He's gonna to give death a run for its money. You wait and see."

There it was again. That smile and this time it sent chills down her spine until she suddenly felt the warmth of Colt's hand on top of hers attempting to comfort her. She jerked her hand back before she realized what she had done. *What am I so afraid of?*

"Here you go, Colt. I think there's enough here to cover what I have on the list. Cassy, I didn't even think to ask if you want Colt to pick you up anything at the store while he is in town." James wheeled his chair close to the table.

"You're welcome to go into town with me, Cassy?" Colt stood up from the table, picked up his cowboy hat and ran his fingers through his hair.

Cassy could feel the room start heating up more, or was it just her.

"That way you can pick up what you need and we'll have a chance to get to know each other."

"That's a great idea, Colt. It's time for me to rest anyway. You don't want to be stuck around the house with nothing to do." James reached up and patted Cassy's shoulder in approval.

"I was going to do some unpacking and then start getting something ready for dinner." Cassy tried to come up with a legitimate excuse to get out of going with him. She certainly didn't like his comment about not being needed on the farm, but in a strange way she was overwhelmed by the way he was making her feel.

"Oh, go on. You'll have more fun going into town with Colt." Before James moved his wheelchair back a little, he placed his tote containing his blood tester, test strips and insulin that were lying on the table on his lap. "But before you go Cassandra, will you help me into the bedroom?"

"I'll be happy to Grandpa." Cassy didn't look at Colt before she began pushing her grandfather into his bedroom. She didn't want to know what he was doing with that smile. "Are you sure you'll be all right while I'm gone?"

"I'll be fine. I've learned to be alone since your Grandma passed. You go and have a good time. See if anything's changed in town since the last time you were here. I'll see you when you get back."

"Okay then." Cassy helped her grandfather into bed placing his tote on the nightstand next to his bed. She made sure his cane was close enough for him to reach if he needed it. "I'll go into town with Colt, but I won't be long. You have a nice rest and I'll check in on you when I return. I love you Grandpa." She kissed him on the forehead.

"I love you too, Cassandra. I'm really glad you're here."

Cassy watched as he made himself comfortable on the bed, placing his tote next to him so he could check his blood. She placed a blanket next to him on the bed in case he wanted cover.

"You know Cassandra, Colt's right. Your name's beautiful and so are you."

"Thank you, Grandpa." She touched his hand. "Have a nice rest."

Cassy stopped in her bedroom to freshen her makeup. She grabbed her purse from her bed and walked back into the kitchen. "I'm ready if you are."

"Great. Let's go." Colt put his cowboy hat on and motioned Cassy to go ahead of him but stayed in step close behind her. She walked out the backdoor as Colt held it open. As she passed, she noticed his musky scent and felt the heat from his body close to hers.

"My truck's right over here."

Cassy watched Colt sprint ahead of her and open the passenger door, holding her arm as she climbed inside. She sank in the seat of his truck and watched as he slid in behind the wheel. She couldn't help but laugh. If someone had told her a week ago she would be in Oklahoma in the truck of an Adonis named Colt Matthews heading into town for supplies, she would have never believed them. Her world had definitely turned on its axle.

CHAPTER THREE

"That should be all. Are you ready to head back?" Colt pushed the cart down the grocery store isle towards the register.

"I think we got everything on the list." Cassy glanced over the list her grandfather made one last time.

"Why don't you go ahead? You have a lot less than I do." Colt held the basket back so Cassy could go ahead of him in line. "What's all that stuff?"

Cassy carefully placed a few items on the register. "Just some make up, shampoo and conditioner. Why?"

"You don't need all that stuff." Colt smiled at Cassy sending another shock through her body. She wished she knew how long it was going to take her to get used to that smile.

"Thank you, Colt." She wasn't quite sure how to answer. "I don't know if I believe you though. All women need a little help."

"It's your money to waste. But if you ask me, you're beautiful just the way you are."

Cassy tried not to let drool fall from the corners of her mouth as she watched Colt lean over, balancing himself with his muscular arms on the handle of the cart. The muscles of his chest pressed against the material of his t-shirt making them more than noticeable. She did her best not to let Colt know what pleasure his body and last comment gave her, she placed her empty small basket on the register along with the items she had removed.

Trying to change the conversation, Cassy asked. "Besides working on the farm, what else do you like to do, Colt? Do you have any hobbies?"

"I ride broncos at rodeos. I'm actually the title holder for the state rodeo." Cassy didn't have a hard time imagining him in his tight jeans, chaps and cowboy hat twisting and turning on top of a bucking bull. In fact, she found the thought exciting her. She was finding herself jealous of the bull.

"Really. That's impressive. Maybe you'll compete sometime soon and Grandpa and I can come and watch."

"I have a competition coming up next month not far away. You're welcome to come then."

"Let me know when it is and I'll see what Grandpa's got planned." Cassy handed money to the cashier and waited for her change.

"You know looking at all this food's making me hungry. How about if we stop at the café down the street and grab a bite before we go back to the farm?" Colt asked.

"I'm actually hungry myself. That sounds good. I bet you don't get to eat out very often since you live on the farm."

"Not often. I take every opportunity I get." Colt watched as the cashier scanned his items and bagged them.

"I remember enjoying every opportunity we had to go to town and eat out when I would stay with Grandpa and Grandmother." Cassy smiled as the memories flooded back.

"I need a couple bags of ice, too." Colt handed the cashier money, took his change and began pushing the cart out the door of the store to his truck.

Cassy followed close beside. "What do they have that's good at the café?" Cassy asked. "I haven't been there in a long time."

"They have a great burger, if you like burgers. They always have the daily special which is guaranteed to put a few pounds on you. It's normally something fried with a biscuit and gravy. Whatever you order you'll like."

Cassy watched Colt began loading the bags in the back of his truck. She liked the way his flexing muscles shimmered from the sun and sweat. He was a nice-looking man, but there still was something Cassy wasn't sure about. She was going to have to get past it because they were going to have to work together if she decided to stay. If she was going to make a go of running the family farm, she needed to trust Colt to get her up to speed.

"I gotta grab the ice. Why don't you load the rest in the cooler?" Colt headed to the ice freezer.

Cassy climbed in the back of Colt's truck to open the lid of the cooler and started loading the dairy items from the bags. Colt returned with two bags of ice and placed them carefully on top of the items in the cooler then shut the lid. He picked up a tarp lying in the back and threw it across the top of the cooler and the rest of the bags.

"That should keep them cold and safe until we get back to the farm. Are you ready to go eat?" Colt asked extending his hand to help Cassy down.

"Yes." Cassy took his hand then climbed down and into the passenger side of the truck.

**

The cafe wasn't busy. Cassy realized she was used to crowds in Texas restaurants. She was going to have to remember where she was and it wasn't a big city in Texas. It was small town Oklahoma.

As they started to take a seat in one of the empty booths, a female voice came from behind them.

"Colt Mathews, what can I get for you?"

"Fannie." Colt replied as they both turned to see a thin, older lady wearing an apron around her waist and a pencil behind her ear walking up behind them.

"We stopped in for lunch. What's your special today?" Colt asked.

Fannie came walking up to the table. "You're looking good there, Colt."

"Thanks, Fannie." When Colt put his massive arms around her and gave her a hug she seemed to disappear.

"Homemade chicken pot pie is the daily special." Fannie managed to get out when Colt finally released her.

"That sounds good, but I think I'll stick with a cheeseburger," Cassy replied as she took a seat in the booth.

"I'll take the same and a cold beer. By the way Fannie, this is Cassy Conner."

"Conner you say. You aren't James Conner's grandkid, are you?" Fannie asked.

"Yes, I am." Cassy smiled. "You know my grandfather?"

"Yes. You forget it's a small town. I heard you were coming to town. Welcome dear. You think you're gonna run the family farm? Didn't your grandfather teach you that's a man's job? Colt here's doing a wonderful job for your grandfather. I don't know why you would want that to change." Fannie kept her eyes locked on Cassy.

Cassy got the distinct impression Fannie was a big fan of Colt Matthews.

"No, he didn't tell me it was a man's job and I didn't say anything was going to change." Cassy corrected her.

"Well, then maybe after you've been here a few weeks, you find out it's hard work running a farm. I'm sure it's not quite the job you had in Texas, but then you lost that job, didn't you?" Fannie shot Cassy a slight grin. "If you decide you want a woman's job, I can always use some help around the café."

Cassy looked at Colt for some help with the conversation. He shrugged his shoulders and smiled that crooked little smile.

"I'll keep that in mind, Fannie." Cassy wasn't sure exactly where Fannie's attitude towards her was coming from. She decided to let it pass this time. Next time she would be more on the defense.

"Sure, Deary. You just let me know."

Cassy laughed as Fannie disappeared behind the counter to pour their beer.

"Thanks for all the help there, Colt." Cassy snapped. "Fannie's one strong willed, opinionated woman who I believe likes you a lot. She's also under the impression I'm coming here to take your job from you. I wonder where she would get an idea like that." Cassy leaned forward. She noticed a slight grin beginning on Colt's face as he rubbed his fingers across his lips to try and hide it.

"I come in here as much as I can. Fannie's easy to talk to. In fact, I thought about fixin' your grandfather up with her. I think they would hit it off, don't you?"

"Don't do me any favors, please," Cassy replied. "She already doesn't like me. If I didn't know better, I would think she's trying to protect you from me."

Cassy could feel her pulse quicken and a shock run through her body as Colt took her hands in his and moved in close. This time she was not going to give him the satisfaction of knowing he made her uncomfortable by pulling her hand away. After all she was enjoying the view. He had the most beautiful deep dark brown eyes and a solid chin to support the striking features of his face. He still had a little stubble on his cheeks which Cassy liked.

"You're going to need a strong, capable man to protect you. I'm available."

Cassy couldn't quit looking into his eyes and she certainly couldn't say anything.

Colt finally let go of her hand as Fannie returned placing their beers on the table in front of them.

"Aren't you two cozy? Your burgers will be out in a few. Is there anything else you two need?"

"We're fine Fannie. Thank you." Colt smiled at Cassy. As if his touch didn't send her over the edge, there was that smile again.

The rest of lunch was almost complete silence. Cassy knew Colt realized he had gotten to her mentally and excited her physically. That was the last thing she wanted was him to know he could make her weak.

"It was nice to meet you. Fannie." Colt noticed Cassy gave him an *I'm trying to be nice* stare as she headed for the door. "I'll wait for you outside, Colt."

"I'll be out as soon as I settle up here with Fannie."

Cassy could feel Colt watching her walk out the front door.

CHAPTER FOUR

"What do I owe you?"

"I'm over here." Fannie chuckled as she waved her hand in front of Colt's face drawing his attention away from Cassy walking out the door.

He felt his face turn red. He knew he had been caught checking Cassy out, but it was worth it.

"You know what they say about fishin' off the company dock?" Fannie raised her eyebrows as she glared at Colt. "Here's your total." She handed him a ticket. "I know you probably want a receipt since you're covering the bill for the boss' granddaughter. I'm sure you can write it off on your taxes."

"That's why I love you, Fannie. You're always taking care of me." Colt gave her a wink.

"Remember that, would you, especially when I tell you to be careful around this one. Cassy seems like one you don't want to mess with."

"Who says I want anything to do with her? She's the granddaughter of my boss. I'd be stupid to try anything." Colt's thoughts returned to her legs and her mouth, hot and most, pressed up against his.

"I know you Colt Matthews. You like a challenge." Fannie laughed.

"You do know me Fannie, probably too well." Colt handed Fannie money. "Keep the change."

"Thanks, Hun. You have yourself a good day. Don't let it be so long before we see you again."

"I'll try Fannie. It's always a pleasure." Colt tipped his cowboy hat, headed out the front door of the café and met Cassy standing by the truck.

"Are you ready to head back to the farm?" Colt unlocked the truck door and opened it for Cassy. He watched when she climbed in the passenger side. Her shorts moving up her silky legs as she sat down in the truck seat. Shutting the door, Colt noticed the outline of her breast as she clipped the seatbelt around her.

"Not bad." He whispered as he walked around the truck to the driver's side.

"Is everything all right?" Cassy asked.

"Yeah, why?" Colt climbed into the truck and shut the door.

"I thought I heard you say something."

"Sorry. I didn't say a thing." Colt smiled. "Let's head back." He started the truck and back out of the parking spot. "Did you enjoy lunch?"

"It was good. Thank you, by the way, for buying. Next time it's my turn."

"So, there's going to be a next time?" Colt smiled at the thought. "It's a date."

"I don't think you would call it a date." Cassy exclaimed. "I'm sure there'll be plenty of times we can come into town together to pick up supplies."

"Of course." Colt grinned. "We wouldn't want anyone in town to know we were dating." Colt could tell by the look on Cassy's face he was frustrating her. There was nothing he enjoyed more than to know he was making someone uncomfortable, especially a beautiful woman.

"Stop it Colt. You know what I mean."

"I'm just teasing you Cassy. Don't take everything I say so seriously."

"Fine."

Colt watched out of the corner of his eye as Cassy adjusted herself in the seat and crossed her arms in front of her. He had gotten to her and it made him happy. He could feel the excitement rushing through his body. He was going to have to learn her limits so he would know how far to push her comfort level. Fannie was right he enjoyed a challenge.

CHAPTER FIVE

Cassy picked up a few of the packages from the back of the truck and carried them in the kitchen. The house was quiet. They were gone longer than they planned. Her grandfather should be awake by now. Heading towards the bedroom to check on him, Cassy didn't want him to sleep past dinner.

"Grandpa, how are you doing?" Cassy sat down on the edge of the bed. Her grandfather didn't respond. His breathing was shallow. Taking his hand in hers, he was clammy. Sweat covered his forehead. Running to the kitchen, Cassy yelled out the back door. "Something's not right. Colt. Help me."

"What's wrong Cassy." Colt asked as he walked up to the back door.

"Something's wrong with Grandpa. He's not waking up." Cassy ran back to the bedroom with Colt following right behind her.

"Let me check." Feeling his neck for a pulse, Colt turned to Cassy. "His pulse is faint. Call 911."

Cassy dialed 911 on the phone next to her grandfather's bed. "My grandfather needs help. He's diabetic and not responding." She recited her grandfather's name and address before hanging up the phone. "They should be here soon."

"He's not conscience enough to eat or drink juice to bring up his sugars."

Cassy watched Colt open and look through the drawer in the nightstand next to the bed. He pulled out a red box. She remembered seeing her Grandmother do the same thing. Taking what looked like a pin out of the case, Colt gave her grandfather a shot.

"What did you give him?" Cassy asked.

"I gave him a glucose shot to help bring up his blood sugar levels. It takes a few minutes to start working. Hopefully by the time the ambulance arrives."

Those few minutes seemed like an eternity to Cassy. She ran to the kitchen door after hearing the sirens coming up the road. Waiting for them grab their medical bags from the ambulance, she opened the door to show them the way. One of the paramedics ran in front of her making his way directly to her grandfather's bedroom.

"How's he doing Colt?"

"Lucas. He's still out of it." Colt moved away from the bed so Lucas could sit down. "I gave him a glucose shot just about a minutes ago."

"That should help." Lucas turned towards Cassy. "Who are you?"

"I'm his granddaughter," Cassy replied.

"You're Mr. Conner's granddaughter? What's your name granddaughter?"

"Cassy. My name is Cassy." She stood back out of the way, nervously wringing her hands.

"It's nice to meet you Cassy, I'm Lucas. Lucas Harding. I'd shake your hand but I'm a little occupied." He looked up at her and for the first time since he arrived.

Cassy caught a glimpse of the most gorgeous man she had seen in a long time. Well, at least since she met Colt Matthews. His eyes were robin's egg blue and his dark, thick eyelashes framed his oval eyes perfectly. Cassy watched as he took her grandfather's blood pressure and checked his pulse. After a few minutes he checked his blood sugar levels.

"Mr. Conner. It's Lucas. You remember me, don't you? Mr. Conner." Lucas turned to Cassy. "Did he have a snack this afternoon?"

"We had some milk and cookies a few hours ago. I made sure they were sugar free. That's all I know he has eaten since I got here."

"It sure looks like he took a little too much insulin. He'll be all right in a few minutes. It's a good thing you found him when you did." Lucas stayed right with him until he began to come around. Checking him every few minutes to make sure his body was responding properly.

Cassy's heart continued to beat fast as she waiting for her grandfather to begin coming around. She felt Colt's hand on her back which helped calm her.

Lucas left the bedroom for the kitchen bringing back a glass of milk and a banana. He sat back down next to James on the bed. "Here you go Mr. Conner. Drink some of this milk."

Her grandfather's hands were still shaky but he took the glass of milk and began to drink. Cassy watched as Lucas carefully peeled the skin of the banana back.

"Here, how about I trade you." Lucas took the glass of milk and handed James the banana. "Try eating some of this."

The paramedic on the other side of James, checked his blood again and nodded his head up and down at Lucas.

"It looks like you're getting back to normal, Mr. Conner. That's great. Why don't you finish at least half of that banana? Cassy and I need to talk for a few minutes?" Lucas stood up from the bed, took Cassy by the arm and headed out the bedroom door.

"You were wonderful with him. Thank you so much," Cassy replied.

"Do you know how to take care of his diabetes? What to feed him and how to help him count his carbohydrates?" Lucas asked. "I know Colt can help him, but he's not always around. He's normally working around the farm."

"No, not really. I just know my grandmother wouldn't let him have sweets." Cassy grinned. "I would catch him sneaking a candy bar now and then. She always had him eat lots of chicken, fish and vegetables."

"How about if I go get you some reading material I have in the ambulance. I can stop by sometime and go over it with you, if you like. How long are you going to be here with your grandfather?" Lucas asked.

"I'll be here for a while. I just arrived today," Cassy replied.

"Nice welcome." Lucas sighed. "Right now, why don't you sit with your grandfather while I go get that information."

Cassy watched as Lucas walked out the door. She had two gorgeous hunks of men at her disposal. Nancy and Laura weren't going to believe her. She headed back into the bedroom and sat down on the edge of the bed by her grandfather. "You really gave me a scare Grandpa."

"I'm sorry. It's just sometimes I take too much insulin. We ate those cookies so I took a little extra insulin. It must've been too much. Since you're here maybe you can help me keep track of my food. I know sometimes I'm not as careful as I need to be."

"I'll be happy too. You, Colt and Lucas are going to have to teach me what to do. I'm a quick learner." Cassy smiled at him. She could tell he was still trying to regain his composure.

"I'll teach you everything I know. After that, you'll have to ask Lucas. He's very knowledgeable about medical stuff." James laid his head back on his pillow and closed his eyes.

"I noticed. It seems like he's been here a few times. He's pretty familiar with your condition."

"Yes, he's been here a time or two. He works hard just like Colt here." James pointed to Colt. "They don't make 'em like those two anymore."

"They sure don't." Cassy glanced at Colt.

"It looks like you're in good hands, Mr. Conner. I'm going to go back to unloading the truck and then get back to work." Colt walked over to the bed and placed his hand on James' shoulder.

"Thanks for being here, Colt." James patted his hand.

"Anytime, Mr. Conner."

Cassy watched as Colt walked out the bedroom door. "Let me get you a dry shirt and then, if you feel like it, we can go into the kitchen and get you some more milk and something else to eat. I can put the supplies away while you tell me where they go. I want to keep you where I can see you."

"Sounds like a deal to me."

Cassy found a shirt in his closet. She helped him change then out of his bed and into his wheelchair.

"I'm glad you're here, Cassandra. I need you right now." James reached back and patted her hand.

Cassy leaned down and hugged her grandfather. "I'm glad I'm here too. I can't think of anywhere else I would rather be."

Putting the groceries away, Cassy watched as her grandfather sat at the kitchen table having a bowl of low sugar ice cream.

"Looks like you're feeling better and found something to eat." Lucas sat down at the table next to James.

"Can't beat a good bowl of ice cream, even if it's not the real stuff. You want some?" James held up his almost empty bowl.

"No thanks, Mr. Conner. I'm just leaving some information for your granddaughter and then I have to get back to work. I promised Cassy I would stop by sometime and you and I would go over with her how to count your carbohydrates and how she can help you take care of your diabetes."

"That's nice of you Lucas. When do you get off work?" James asked.

"I should get off around five tonight. That is if we don't have any calls that keep me out."

"Why don't you stop by after work and have dinner with Cassandra and me? How does some baked chicken and vegetables sound?" James asked. "Maybe a nice green salad."

"That sounds really good Mr. Conner, but I don't want to impose. I can stop by sometime tomorrow, when it's a little more convenient."

"Nonsense. You're welcome to stop by for dinner tonight. Right Cassandra?"

"Right Grandpa." Cassy smiled. "You're more than welcome to join us for dinner. It's no trouble at all."

"In that case, I would love to. It would be nice to have a home cooked meal." Lucas smiled at Cassy.

Cassy thought she was going to melt into the linoleum on the floor. This time it wasn't the fact it was ninety degrees outside, it was the look in Lucas' eyes. Colt's smile and Lucas' eyes. She was in way over her head.

"I've got to get back to work now. I guess I'll see the two of you around five." Lucas walked towards the door. "Make sure he behaves himself until then."

"I will," Cassy replied. "Thank you again, Lucas."

She just realized one of the most handsome men in the state of Oklahoma was coming to dinner tonight. There were no restaurants to grab take out, no place to call that delivers edible cuisine.

"How hard can it be to make a salad and bake some chicken?"

CHAPTER SIX

Cassy finished putting the last of the groceries away. After a day like today, she needed to soak in a nice calming bath before she started cooking dinner. It'd been a long day of traveling, taking a trip into town with Colt and then her grandfather having a problem with his blood sugar. A bath would be the perfect answer and now would be the perfect time. Colt came back to the house to check on her grandfather and they were going over business at the kitchen table.

"Since you guys are occupied, I'm going to take a quick bath before I start dinner. Colt, you're coming to dinner, right? Grandpa invited Lucas. You're welcome to join us. I might as well give all three of you food poisoning."

"Sure, why not. That sounds amazing."

Cassy saw his eyes light up as he laughed. "Great. Lucas will be here around five. Why don't you come back then if you aren't still here going over business?" Cassy waved as she headed to towards the bathroom.

"Don't get all dolled up for me Cassy." Colt yelled behind her.

"Don't worry Colt. If I get dolled up, it won't be for you." She was going to get all dolled up, but it was going to be for her. She deserved it after today. It did cross her thoughts that both Lucas and Colt would be here for dinner.

Sticking her big toe up against the faucet made the running water spray out against the side of the tub. Cassy could hear her grandmother voice.

Cassandra stop doing that or you're going to get your toe stuck in the faucet and we'll have to cut it off.

She never asked if her grandmother meant her toe or the water faucet. She laid her head back on the edge of the tub. This was the first chance she'd gotten to relax since she arrived. It felt good.

She found her mind wandering, thinking about Lucas. He was so easy to talk to. Normally she was tongue tied and fidgety around guys she just met. For some reason Lucas didn't make her feel that way at all. She was at ease with him. Maybe it was because he was so good with her grandfather that made her fell so comfortable around him. It didn't hurt that she found him attractive.

Then there was Colt. His smile sent sparks through her body. She went straight from comfortable to aching for his touch which made her feel a little uncomfortable. Her guard was up with him since he enjoyed pushing her buttons.

Cassy was looking forward to seeing Lucas again even if Colt was going to be there, too. She could pull this off. She could manage to have dinner with both of them and not have a problem. Her grandfather would be there to help the situation. Hopefully Colt would behave himself and allow all of them to enjoy the evening.

****

Cassy removed the chicken out of the refrigerator along with the lettuce and salad dressing.

"How about if you let me cook the chicken on the grill since it's so hot? It won't heat up the house and you can make the rest of the meal. Sound like a deal?" Colt asked as he walked through the back door and put his hand on her grandfather's shoulder who was sitting at the kitchen table reading.

"Sounds good to me. Are you sure?" Cassy placed the chicken on a platter and seasoned it with salt and pepper.

"I grill a mean chicken. Wait and see. Besides I want to make it through the meal without getting sick."

Cassy tried not to look at him because she knew there would be that smile on his face which would distract her. Then there was his hair. The way it fell back into place perfectly after he ran his fingers though. She noticed he had taken his hat off and hung it on the back of one of the kitchen chairs after he walked in the door which meant he had run his fingers through his hair already. She had missed that.

"I hate to make you work since we invited you over for dinner."

"It's not a problem. I'll go get it started and come back in to see if there's anything else I can help you with."

"It's ready when you are. I'll start the vegetables and set the table." Cassy handed Colt the platter of chicken.

"It's gonna to be nice to have a woman around the house again isn't Mr. Conner?" Colt commented as he put his hat on and walked out the kitchen door. "Hi, Lucas."

"I hope I'm not late." Lucas walked through the door as Colt walked out.

"You're right on time Lucas. Come on in." James motioned for him to sit down at the table.

"Colt just went to put the chicken on the grill. Would you like something to drink Lucas?" Cassy asked.

"I'd love a beer, if you have one." Lucas took a seat at the table near James.

"I think there are some in refrigerator. Why don't you help yourself?" Cassy started washing the head of lettuce and tearing it apart.

"I'll take one out to Colt and keep him company while he grills." Lucas stood and made his way to the refrigerator.

Cassy watched Lucas twist the tops off two beers and head out the back door. "Those two seem to be chummy. Are they friends?"

"You forget it's a small-town, Cassy. Everyone knows everyone. Colt and Lucas are two single guys. They have a lot in common," James replied.

"They're completely different. I don't see what they have in common at all except they're around the same age."

"What do you mean?" James looked confused.

"Well, they're both nice looking, I'll give them that. But from what I can tell, Colt's a man's man and hard to predict. Lucas, on the other hand, is a laid-back, nice person."

"I don't know what makes you think that about Colt. He's a good guy. You just have to get to know him. I'm sure he'll be different when he gets to know you. I agree with you about Lucas, though. He's a great kid."

Cassy finished chopping the lettuce and cutting up a tomato and cucumber from the garden. She didn't want to get into the discussion with her grandfather about how Colt took every opportunity since she met him to put her on edge or make her uncomfortable with the next thing he said.

She tossed salad dressing in the salad and placed it on the table. The green beans were cooking on the stove. She cut up some bacon to mix with them and put some red potatoes in a pot of water to cook. Everything smelled wonderful, but needed a little bit longer.

"Just enough time to check on the guys and see how the chicken is coming." Cassy washed her hands and headed out the back door.

****

Lucas helped Cassy clear off the table and put the leftovers away after dinner. "Everything was very good. Thanks for having me to dinner. I know your grandfather inviting me took you by surprise."

"A little, but that's Grandpa for you." Cassy laughed. "He's been that way since I've known him. There's never a stranger or someone who isn't welcome at the dinner table. My grandmother was always making more food than she needed because she never knew how many she would feed."

"I bet you miss her?" Lucas took handed Cassy another bowl of leftovers to go in the refrigerator.

"I do. It's not the same coming to visit." Cassy put the bowl away. "I think that's it. Thanks for the help." She glanced at the table where Colt and her grandfather were talking business.

Cassy and Lucas joined them so they could go over everything James had for dinner, counting the carbohydrates he ate. Even the bowl of ice cream he enjoyed before dinner. Lucas showed Cassy how to count the carbohydrates in James' dinner. He prepared a needle with the right amount of insulin and handed it to Cassy to administer the shot.

"I don't know if I can do this." Cassy looked at the needle.

"You can't hurt him." Lucas explained. "It needs to go in a muscle not in a vein. A good place to give him the shot is in his thigh or in his stomach around his bellybutton. You just pinch a little skin and stick the needle in."

Cassy still couldn't bring herself to do it.

"Here, I'll guide you." Lucas took her hand and stuck the needle in James' thigh then pushed as the insulin flowed from the needle into his leg. "That wasn't so hard right?"

"Not really," Cassy scrunched up her nose. "I'll have to try it again to make sure."

"It's better is he takes his shot before he has dinner, so if you know what he'll be having, you can give him his shot before he begins to eat." Lucas explained.

"If you guys are through using me as a pin cushion, I'm going to go get ready for bed." James smiled as he turned his wheelchair around and headed for his bedroom. "Make sure the kitchen's all cleaned up before you guys turn in for the night."

"Good night, Grandpa. I love you. I'll see you in the morning." Cassy waved at her grandfather as he made his way to his bedroom. "I'll come in and check on you before I go to bed."

"Good night, Cassandra. I love you, too. Good night, Lucas. See you tomorrow, Colt."

"Good night, Mr. Conner. I'll be here to have breakfast with you bright and early tomorrow morning." Colt winked at Cassy. "I guess I'm going to call it a night also. How about you Lucas?"

"I want to go over a few more things with Cassy and then I'll be leaving." Lucas stood up and shook Colt's hand. "It was good to see you again, Colt."

"You too. Thanks for the beer and your help with the chicken." Colt ran his fingers through his hair and put on his cowboy hat. "I'll see you in the morning, Cassy."

"Good night, Colt." Cassy watched him disappear out the kitchen door. She was finally alone with Lucas. Now maybe she could get to know him better. Colt had been watching them the entire night.

"You're really good with Grandpa. It's nice to know you've been around the last few years to take care of him."

"I'm kinda fond of the old man. He reminds me of my grandfather." Lucas sat back down at the table.

"Where is your family?" Cassy asked.

"I only have my mother left. My grandparents died when I was a child. My father took off when I was two or so. I've never knew him."

"That had to be hard." Cassy noticed Lucas' expression turn solemn. "Is your Mom around here?"

"Sort of. She's in a nursing home in town. She has dementia. I try to visit as much as I can, but she doesn't even know me." The expression on his face wasn't the carefree Lucas she was used to but one of deep thought and hurt.

"I'm sorry. I can't imagine. That must be painful."

"Don't be sorry. Every now and then she'll remember and it's worth the wait." Lucas attempted a half-smile.

Cassy could see as he talked about his mother how much he loved her.

"It's probably time for me to leave. I have to be at work early tomorrow." Lucas stood from the table.

Cassy walked with him to his truck while she tried to keep up a conversation. "I'm glad you could come to dinner. I've enjoyed our talk."

"Me too." Lucas agreed. "Thank you for everything, Cassy. Maybe we can do it again sometime?"

"I would love that." Cassy smiled.

"Great. Well, I have to go. Let me give you my cell phone number so if you need anything, you can call me. Anything at all." Lucas pulled a card out of his wallet and handed it to Cassy.

"Thank you. I'll make sure and call if I need to."

"You can also call just because. I wouldn't mind that at all."

The sparkle in his eyes when he smiled made him knockout gorgeous. "I might just do that." Cassy enjoyed the thought of seeing him again or just talking to him on the phone if she needed to hear another person's voice. She missed her friends already.

"I better go. Thanks again."

As Lucas climbed in the pickup and drove away, Cassy headed back to the house. Closing and locking the doors before she went to bed, she stopped and checked on her grandfather. He seemed to be sleeping peacefully. He was breathing normally and his color was good. If she didn't know better, she could swear he was smiling. She bent down and kissed him lightly on the forehead. "I love you, grandpa."

Cassy held the card Lucas had given her tightly in her hand, running her fingers over the raised lettering. She found a safe place for it in the top drawer of her nightstand. Slipping into her nightgown, she climbed into bed. She was going to have no trouble finding something or someone to dream about tonight.

CHAPTER SEVEN

Hey, what's going on?" Cassy asked as she walked into the kitchen. "The sun isn't even up and you guys are in here making all kinds of noise."

"Good morning to you too, sunshine." James Conner smiled. "You're going to have to get used to early hours if you're going to run this farm."

"Good morning, Cassy," Colt replied.

"Come on, Grandpa, you don't have to get up before the crack of dawn to run a farm. This isn't a dairy farm. You've always been an early riser." Cassy sat down at the table and laid her head down. "I remember Grandmother saying she couldn't keep you in bed past six o'clock if she wanted to."

"You can sleep when your dead is what I always say. Why don't you go get in your work clothes and Colt and I'll make you some breakfast?"

"Sure, I'll get dressed." Cassy stood up and headed out the kitchen door. "I'll take my eggs over easy."

Heading to the bedroom, Cassy slipped on a pair of jeans and a t-shirt. She sat down on the bed while she brushed her hair and pulled it back in a ponytail. She opened the drawer of the nightstand next to the bed and took out the business card Lucas gave her last night. Falling asleep thinking about Lucas and how she was looking forward to seeing him again was nice, but somehow during the night her dreams turned to Colt. Why would they turn to him? She tried her best to keep Colt out of her thoughts. Somehow, he kept working his way back in. She finished her hair and headed back to the kitchen.

"Here you go." Colt placed a plate of eggs, bacon and toast down on the table. "Over easy just like you ordered."

"These look great. Thanks Colt." Cassy joined her grandfather at the table. Colt brought her a glass of milk and placed it on the table.

"Wow, the service is better here than it was yesterday at the café and I'm not getting the third-degree from Fannie." Cassy smiled at Colt. "I guess I need to leave you a tip."

"Feel free." Colt smiled. "Or you can pay me back by making dinner tonight then, after dinner, we can go into town and go dancing at local dance hall. You know how to line dance don't you?"

"Dancing? I haven't been line dancing in a long time." Cassy took a bite of her eggs. "That sounds like fun, but I'm going to have to pass. Yesterday was a long day. I'd like to spend tonight around the house. Thank you for the invitation though."

"You two kids go into town and have a good time." James waved a hand in the air. "Don't feel like you have to stick around the house and take care of an old man. I'll be fine."

"That's not it at all, Grandpa. I need to catch up on my sleep from the past few days and I'd like to have a nice quiet night. How about if I get a rain check, Colt?"

"Sure Cassy. We'll find other weekend."

Cassy began to wonder much how fun it would be to spend some time with Colt. She also thought it would be nice to be alone with Lucas. She was totally confused about her feelings. Lucas was sexy, sweet, and gorgeous. Then there was Colt, strong, manly, and ruggedly handsome.

Going dancing with Colt would give her a chance to spend some time alone with him and get to know him better. Her nervousness around him showed. He knew he kept her on edge. Then again, it was a small town. Maybe they would run into Lucas. What else do people have to do around here on a Saturday night? Hopefully they were enjoying themselves and not trying to catch up on their sleep like she planned on doing.

****

Cassy cleaned up the kitchen after Colt and her grandfather were kind enough to make her breakfast. When she finished, she decided to take a trip around the farm. She wanted to see all the changes Colt had made that her grandfather couldn't stop talking about.

"Grandpa, do you want to go for a ride around the farm?" Cassy asked as she grabbed one of her grandmother's hats from the mud room, slipped her cell phone in her pocket and picked up the truck keys. She walked into the living room "How about it? I need a tour guide."

"Sure. It's been awhile since I've been out in the fields. Let's go take a look." Cassy rolled his wheelchair into the kitchen and handed him his cane.

"It's going to be a hot one today. We won't be gone very long." Cassy helped her grandfather slowly walk to the truck, helped him in and then climbed in the driver's side. "This reminds me of old times. You would always take me with you when you went out to inspect the fences or check the crops."

"You loved it when your grandmother would make us lunch and we would spend the whole day in the fields. Those were good times, Cassandra. I loved every minute we spent together."

"Me too, Grandpa." Cassy reached across the seat and patted his hand. "Me too."

"You know this farm is a lot to handle. If something happens to me, I don't want to see you tied do to this lifestyle," James said.

"Don't talk that way Grandpa. You'll be around for a long time to come."

"Cassandra, we need to talk about this. I want you to know you don't have to hang on to the farm when I'm gone. I'm leaving it to you, but that doesn't mean you have to live here and keep it running. There are lots of people around town who would love to buy it from you."

"I know. What if I promise you I'll give it some serious thought?"

"I guess that's all I can ask. I don't want you staying here because you think it's what I want you to do. I want you to be happy. That's all I ever wanted for you. This was my dream and I don't want you to feel a sense of obligation to me."

"Thank you, Grandpa. I promise if I'm not happy running the farm, I'll sell it and find something else to do."

Cassy turned the truck off the gravel road and onto a dirt road. "Can we still go this way for a little while and check out the fences?"

"Sure. When you get down to the end of this road take a right. I want to show you some of the things Gus Thompson and his sons have done to their farm house. You remember Gus' youngest went to college and learned architecture?"

"I remember you telling me that." Cassy nodded.

"Well when he got done, he talked his other brother, who was working construction in Dallas, into helping him remodel their parent's home." James chuckled.

Cassy couldn't remember the last time she heard her grandfather laugh.

"I can't wait for you to see it. It looks like something from outer space. Gus hates it, but would never tell his son or wife."

Cassy turned right like her grandfather had asked.

"It's right up here." James pointed out the truck window.

"Is that it?" Cassy asked as she pulled into the driveway and headed closer to the house.

"Yep, that's it. What do you think?" James smiled

"You were right. It looks like a spaceship." Cassy put her arms over the steering wheel and glared out the front windshield. "Why would they let him change their house into that?"

"James Conner."

Cassy heard a man's voice coming from the barn on the far end of the driveway.

"Hi, Gus. What's new with you?" James asked.

Cassy waved to Gus. "Hello, Mr. Thompson." She stepped out of the truck to shake his hand.

"Welcome home, Cassandra. I heard you were coming back to visit your Grandfather for a while," Gus Thompson replied.

"Yes, I did."

"That's great. So, what are you two doing down this direction?" Gus asked.

"Grandpa wanted to show me your house. He said your sons did some remodeling." Cassy looked at her grandfather and his hand was fisted except for his thumb pointed straight up in the air. Cassy guessed she was covering nicely.

"What do you think about it, Cassy?" Gus asked.

"It's different, Mr. Thompson. You must be proud."

"Yes ma'am. By the way James, I artificially inseminated my cow and everything's going great."

"I'm glad you're pleased, Gus. Let me know when you decide to use my prize bull's stud service again."

"I will. That the best fifty thousand dollars I've spent. I'll be in touch," Gus replied. "Would you like a tour of the house Cassandra?"

"If Grandfather and I weren't in a hurry to get back to the house I'd take you up on it."

"You come back anytime and bring James. I'll give you a tour." Gus nodded in James' direction.

"I'll do that. It was nice to see you again, Mr. Thompson." Cassy climbed in the truck and backed it out of the driveway heading home.

"You were right. That was the strangest looking house I've seen." Cassy noticed her grandfather had become very quiet. He wasn't smiling and laughing like before.

"Grandpa, are you all right?"

"Yes, I'm fine. I was just thinking about something. Let's head back home."

"I thought we were going to look at the rest of the farm?" Cassy couldn't understand his change in plans.

"We can finish up tomorrow. Right now, I want to go back to the house and check out some paperwork."

"Something I can help with?" Cassy asked.

"Maybe. I'm not sure what's going on myself."

CHAPTER EIGHT

Cassy pulled up to the house and helped her grandfather out of the truck, back into the house and into his wheelchair. "It's about time for lunch. Would you like me to make you a sandwich? I'm a little hungry myself."

"I'd like that. How about a ham sandwich?" James asked as he rolled into the front room. "Call me when it's ready."

"Sure." Cassy watched him roll up to his desk in the front room and start flipping through pages in a notebook he had found in the desk. She started making them sandwiches and tried to keep an eye on what he was doing. She poured both of them a glass of iced tea and put the sandwiches on the kitchen table then walked into the front room.

"Your sandwich is done. Are you ready to eat?"

"Sure. I'm starving."

Cassy watched as he closed the notebook and put it in a drawer in the desk. She might just have to do some nosing around when he rested this afternoon.

Helping her grandfather count the carbohydrates and take his shot, they ate their sandwiches in quiet. She cleaned up the kitchen as her grandfather sat at the table looking out the window.

"I think I'll go lay down for a little while. Have you got plans for the afternoon?" James finally broke his silence.

"Nothing really. I have some emails to answer and I need to return some calls to my friends. I'll be around the house if you need me." Cassy gave her grandfather a kiss and helped him wheel into his bedroom and lay down on the bed.

"I was thinking we could have some soup and salad for dinner tonight. I'll make some beef stew. How does that sound?" Cassy adjusted the wheelchair so he could get out of bed when he woke.

"Sounds good to me. I'm glad you're here Cassy. It's great to have you around."

"Thanks Grandpa. I'm glad I'm here too. Have a nice rest."

Cassy walked back to the kitchen and waited until her grandfather was asleep then sat down at the living room desk to find the notebook he was thumbing through earlier.

"Let's see what we can find."

The pages were full of names, addresses, and phone numbers each seemed to have a special number, which from what Cassy could tell, was an identifiable number. Across the top of the page was written A/I Clients.

All Cassy could tell was the notes must have something to do with the farm because it was kept together with all the other books to do with business. She had an idea what she was finding, but decided she would question her grandfather a little further when he woke.

"Where's Mr. Conner."

Cassy was startled by Colt's voice from behind her. She turned to see him removing his cowboy hat and running his fingers through his hair.

"Colt, don't sneak up on me like that." Cassy placed her hand on her chest "You almost scared me to death."

"Sorry about that. I thought you would hear me when I opened the screen door. It has that squeak you can hear from anywhere. You must have been really enthralled in what you were reading."

"Grandpa's laying down for a rest. What do you need?" Cassy asked.

"I wanted to talk to him for a minute. It's nothing important."

Cassy continued putting the books back where her grandfather kept them. She could feel Colt's eyes watching her.

"What are you looking for?" Colt asked.

"Nothing really." Cassy reached back into the desk and took out the notebook. "Wait, maybe you can help me."

"Sure, with what?"

"We were out driving around the farm today. Grandpa wanted to show me the Thompson's house. While we were there, Mr. Thompson and Grandpa were talking about the prize bull stud service. For some reason Grandpa got really quiet and wanted to head home."

"What's so strange about that?" Colt asked.

"I'm not sure, but when we got home, Grandpa came straight in here and was looking at this notebook." Cassy handed the notebook to Colt. "Is there something there you see that's out of place?"

Cassy watched as Colt thumbed through the notebook.

"I don't see anything strange. Nothing at all." He handed the notebook back to Cassy. "He acted strange, huh? Did Gus say something to your grandfather?"

"Just that he was thinking about using the stud service again. It was the best fifty thousand dollars he had ever spent."

"There's nothing strange about that." Colt paused for a minute. "Would you tell Mr. Conner I need to go into town to get a part for the tractor? Since it's late. I'll probably grab dinner in town so I'll be back late."

"Sure, I'll tell him." Cassy nodded.

"Also, tell him I would like to sit down and talk to you two about the farm. When you can make some time, let me know."

"I'm sure we can make some time," Cassy said.

"Great. Is there anything you need while I'm in town? I'll be happy to pick it up for you."

"I think there might be a few things. Thanks for asking." Cassy stood up from the desk. "Let me get you some money and a list."

She found the list on the kitchen cabinet and took some money out of the cookie jar where her grandfather kept a small stash for occasions like this and handed it to Colt. "That should be enough."

"If you guys are already in bed when I get, I'll slip in and put them on the cabinet."

"Sounds good. Just make sure to lock the door when you leave." Cassy slipped her hands in the back pockets of her jeans.

"Sure." Colt smiled and nodded. "I'll see you tomorrow then. Have a good evening."

"Thanks. Have fun in town. Try to stay out of trouble." Cassy watched Colt run his fingers through his thick, black hair and put on his cowboy hat. He really needed to stop that. It was getting to her.

"Now, that wouldn't be any fun would it?" Colt smiled.

She was sure there had to be plenty of women in town willing to share an evening with Colt Matthews. Cassy was taken by surprise when she suddenly felt a twinge of jealousy rush through her body.

****

"Dinner was wonderful Cassy."

"Thanks Grandpa. Grandmother taught me everything I know. I'm a little out of practice though." Cassy began picking up the dishes from the table and putting them in the sink.

"You know she loved having you here. You were like the daughter she never had." James took a dink of his tea. "I don't know if she ever told you, but your grandmother always wanted a big family. She had problems when she carried your father and after she had him, the doctors told her she wouldn't be able to have any more kids."

"She never told me. I guess I never questioned why she only had one child." Cassy noticed the sadness on her grandfather's face.

"She was pretty upset for a long time and then you came along. You were what she needed to fill the void she had been feeling. She completely forgot about it and was the happiest I'd ever seen her."

Cassy noticed a tear in the corner of her grandfather's eye. "Thank you for telling me that Grandpa." She gave him a hug. "I loved Grandmother too."

—

"I know you did. Now, how about you help me take my shots?" James reached over and picked up his tote that contained his insulin.

"It would be my pleasure." Cassy pulled a chair up next to him at the table and watched as he took the needle and carefully filled it with insulin.

"That should be just about right with what we had for dinner. You agree?" James asked.

"Let see, you had a pretty big bowl of stew and a salad. That should be just right." Cassy smiled. "Can I give you the shot?"

"Sure. Here you go."

Cassy took the needle from her grandfather and gave him the shot in his leg. "That should do it. Now I'm going to finish cleaning up the kitchen."

"I think I'll go into the front room and do some reading. I'll let you know if I turn in for the night."

"By the way, Grandpa, before I forget, Colt wanted to sit down with the two of us. I told him we could make some time." Cassy waited for her grandfather's answer.

"We can make some time tomorrow. Did he say what it was about?" James asked.

"No, he didn't. I guess we wait and see. I am going outside and enjoy the evening. How about if we have some milk and cookies before you go to bed?" Cassy asked as he wheeled into the living room through the kitchen door.

"Sounds wonderful."

"Okay. Go ahead. Leave me alone here to talk to myself. I'll be fine, don't worry," Cassy replied under her breath continuing to clean the kitchen. "This house will be spotless unless I find some other things to do in this town."

CHAPTER NINE

"Hey, Colt." A voice from behind him caused Colt to turn and check out who was talking.

"Lucas." Colt spotted him walking towards him. "What's up?"

"I could ask you the same. It's not normal for you to be in town at night during the week. What errands does old man Conner have you doing now?" Lucas took a seat at Colt's table.

"He doesn't. I had some personal business to take care of." Colt was never quite sure about Lucas, but he'd grown to like him over the past few months. He knew his stuff and seemed to care about James Conner when he'd answered emergency calls at the farm. That was good enough for Colt. Being a paramedic seemed to be a profession Lucas was good at. Colt took the last drink of his beer and sat the glass down on the table.

"How's the old man doing since our last visit? Is his granddaughter helping take care of his diabetes? What was her name Cassy?" Lucas asked.

"He's doing better. Cassy's trying to learn and help him. She'll get there. She's a smart lady."

"So how is it for you to have her around? Are you adjusting to have a woman for a boss now?" Lucas laughed.

"She's not my boss. Not yet. I still answer to Mr. Conner." Colt wasn't sure how he was going to handle having Cassy as a boss if that's how things turned out. "I guess I'll worry about it when it happens."

"She seems really business-like. I wonder what she knows about running a farm." Lucas rubbed the back of his neck.

"I'm not sure what she knows. I don't know how to tell her she's taking on a headache."

"What do you mean? I thought the Conner farm was doing great. Especially since you guys started earning fees for that prize-winning bull old man Conner has."

"Mr. Conner ran up quite a few bills after his wife died and he got sick. While he was taking care of all the medical stuff, I was worrying about the farm." Colt explained.

"So, you're saying the farm isn't doing well?" Lucas asked.

"It was. I began pumping some of my personal money into the farm to keep it afloat until Mr. Conner could get back on his feet. I'm working on getting my money back now we're making a profit. I have to talk to Mr. Conner and Cassy tomorrow and explain what I've done and see how they react." Colt twisted the glass on the table.

"They should be thankful you were there to help him out. Why didn't you call family and let them worry about it?"

"Cassy was the only family I knew of and I had no idea how to find her. When Mr. Conner was sick I couldn't get any information out of him and he didn't want Cassy to worry about him. Using my own funds was all I could think of to keep from him losing everything and me losing my job." Colt explained.

"So how have you been repaying yourself and him not know. Doesn't the old man keep an eye on the books?" Lucas leaned forward placing his elbows on the table.

"I've been raising the fee we're charging for the prize bull and taking the difference as payback. Problem is, I think the old man figured it out today. I need to talk to him before he gets the wrong idea."

"Why would he get the wrong idea?" Lucas asked.

"He might think I'm skimming money by raising the fees. He doesn't understand he was way underpriced in the market. The customers were willing to pay the extra. They didn't even blink an eye. I kept the price where I wasn't ripping anyone off." Colt rubbed the back of his neck.

"I think the old man will understand when you explain it to him. Cassy on the other hand might need some convincing." Lucas shook his head. "Let me know if you need some help with her. She looks like a handful."

"I'll be fine. Cassy's a nice girl. You just have to get to know her."

"I'd like to get to know her. I'd like to get to know her a lot better. I've been thinking about asking her out for dinner. I'm looking forward to seeing what she's got to offer."

Colt changed the subject quickly. He was getting angry with Lucas talking about Cassy that way. For some reason, he felt a strange need to protect her. Colt had enough on his mind. He didn't need to add being mad at Lucas over Cassy. He caught the eye of his waitress and motion for her "Can we get a picture of what's on draft please?"

"It's on me." Lucas handed the waitress a twenty.

"Thanks Lucas. I had a little too much coffee after dinner and a few beers. Nature calls. I'll be right back."

"I'll grab us a pool table." Lucas checked out the young waitress as she sat down the pitcher of beer with two clean glasses and his change. "Thanks. Keep the change." Lucas touched her on the arm running his hand lightly up and down her bare skin. "Why don't I hang around until you get off work? Maybe we can spend some time together."

"What about your friend?" The waitress leaned into him smiling.

"Don't worry about him. He'll be leaving soon." Lucas reached around and grabbed a handful of her buttocks then patted her playfully.

"I'll see what I can do about getting off early."

"Good girl." Lucas smiled as he watched her walk away. "Beautiful. Now to take care of my friend here."

CHAPTER TEN

Still full from dinner, Cassy passed on cookies and milk with her grandfather before bed. Deciding to turn in early, she helped her grandfather to his room, gave him a glass of milk and a few cookies and left his insulin case by his bed for him to take his nightly shot.

She slipped her nightgown on, folded her clothes and put them away before brushing her hair and her teeth before she climbed under the covers. Flipping through the channels on the television she found a show on she wanted to watch and settled in bed. It didn't take very long before she was asleep only to be awaken by strange noises.

Turning off the television, she listened for a more sounds. She heard another noise which seemed to be coming from the kitchen. She looked at the clock which read twelve thirty.

Cassy slipped on her bathrobe and then tip-toed down the hallway. Carefully peaking around the corner of the kitchen door, she noticed Colt placing grocery bags on the cabinet. She was tired and didn't feel like carrying on a conversation so she headed quietly back down the hallway to her room. She climbed back in bed, covered up and went back to sleep.

****

Cassy opened her eyes and glanced at the clock. The sun wasn't quite up yet and she was awake. It didn't take long for her internal alarm to kick in and reset to the crack of dawn.

Cassy climbed out of bed after stretching her arms and legs. She brushed her hair and slipped on her bathrobe and headed toward the kitchen to start breakfast. She glanced in her grandfather's bedroom as she passed noticing he wasn't awake yet. His glass of milk was empty and the cookies were gone. She decided she would let him sleep and made her way to the kitchen.

"Good Morning." Colt walked through the back door and took off his hat hanging it on the back of one of the chairs. "Where's the old man? He's usually up and waiting for me in the morning."

"I was just going to check on him again. I walked by his bedroom earlier and it didn't look like he was awake yet, which isn't like him at all." Cassy hurried down the hallway to his bedroom.

"Grandpa." She sat down on the bed. This time was different. He looked so peaceful. If Cassy didn't know better she could swear he was smiling. She looked at the clock and it read five minutes after six.

"Call 911." She looked up at Colt with tears running down her cheeks. "See if Lucas is on duty and if he can take the call."

Colt picked up the phone and dialed as Cassy held her grandfather's hand. She listened to Colt give all the information to the operator.

"They're on the way. Is he gone?" Colt asked.

"Yes, I think so." Cassy could feel the tears flowing. She wasn't ready to let him go. She felt Colt sit down on the bed behind her and put his arms on her shoulders.

"I'm so sorry, Cassy. I'm really sorry."

—

She couldn't say anything. Everything was so quiet until she heard the sirens in the distance. Colt headed for the backdoor to let them in.

"Cassy." Lucas helped her up from the bed and handed her to Colt to steady. "I need to check him out."

Cassy watched as Lucas tried to find a pulse then checked his breathing. He pulled a flashlight out of his pocket and checked his eyes. He stood up and took Cassy in his arms.

"I'm sorry Cassy. He's gone. It looks like he had been dead for a few hours now."

All she could do was cry. Her knees became weak and her heart began to pound faster. She leaned into Colt and wept. Years of memories flashed before her eyes.

"Why don't we go in the kitchen while we wait for the police and the ambulance to come. They'll take Mr. Conner to the funeral home. Colt can stay here with him. I'm sure they'll want to talk to you when they get here." Lucas helped steadied her as they headed for the kitchen.

Cassy took one last look at her grandfather before she walked out of his bedroom. "He looks so peaceful."

"Yes, he does. I don't think I've seen him smile like that except when he would talk about you," Lucas said.

"I'm going to miss him so much. I can't believe he's gone." Cassy's voice broke.

"He knew you loved him. His life was complete with you here. It'll take time, but everything will be all right. You wait and see."

Cassy sat down in the chair at the table and watched Lucas make his way around the kitchen finding the coffee and filters.

"Was there anything different about him last night? Did he have any problems or seem ill?" Lucas asked.

"No, we had dinner, he took his shot and then he did some reading in the front room. We had milk and cookies before we went to bed. He checked his blood and then we both turned in. Nothing different at all." Cassy thought back through all their movements.

"I'm sure there will be an autopsy and we'll find out exactly what happened. It could've been his heart or anything. I wish I could tell you more, but I don't know for sure."

"I know you're doing the best you can. Thank you for everything, Lucas."

Colt joined them in the kitchen. "I couldn't stay in there any longer with him. It's so strange to see him that way. To not hear him give me a hard time about something."

"How about you Colt, did you notice anything strange about Mr. Conner last night?" Lucas asked.

"No, but I wasn't here. I went into town yesterday and didn't return until after midnight. Everything seemed quiet and normal when I got home," Colt replied.

"If you're all right Cassy, I'm going to go outside and watch for the ambulance." Colt put on his cowboy hat.

"Sure, go ahead." Cassy hadn't thought about how hard this must be on Colt. She had only been thinking of herself. He had worked for her grandfather for over five years now. He had to be hurting also and wondering what's going to happen now.

"Colt, wait." Cassy said. "Thank you for being here."

"Sure Cassy. I'm sorry about Mr. Conner. It's been my pleasure working for him these past five years. It's not going to be the same around here."

Cassy could swear she heard Colt's voice cracking. She wouldn't know for sure because he was out the door before he finished his sentence.

CHAPTER ELEVEN

Cassy still couldn't believe her grandfather was gone. The house was quiet and she was lonely, not sure what to do now. She'd moved here to help her grandfather on the farm. Now he was gone, she was not only alone on the farm, but now the owner.

Lucas offered to drive her into town to plan her grandfather's funeral. She was going to take clothes for him to the funeral home. She'd argued with Colt about what to bury him in. Colt wanted to take a suit and Cassy felt nice shirt and slacks would look more like him. She didn't remember her grandfather wearing a suit except for a few times in her life. She remembered him being uncomfortable each time. How could she make him wear one for eternity? The last thing she wanted was to be buried in a dress. "What a horrible thought." She whispered.

"What's a horrible thought?"

Cassy turned around to see Colt standing in the kitchen putting his cowboy hat on the back of one of the chairs. "Nothing, I was talking to myself."

"I thought I would stop by and see if you needed anything."

"Thank you, Colt, but I'm fine." Cassy paused for a minute. "I'll be fine. It's going to take a while."

"I know what you mean. I expect to see him come wheeling out of the bedroom." Colt sat down at the kitchen table.

"Me too."

"How long are you going to stay here? Now that your grandfather's gone, I expect you'll want to sell the ranch and move back to Texas."

"What makes you think that Colt?" Cassy looked surprised by his question.

"There's nothing keeping you here now. All your family's gone. I just thought."

"You think I'm going to move away. Do you think I'm going to sell the farm?" Cassy asked. "Maybe sell it to you?"

"Not at all." Colt stuttered. "That's not at all what I was thinking. I know you have friends in Texas and I thought you might want to be close to them instead of stickin' around here where you don't know many people." Colt threw his shoulders back. "And what would be wrong with selling the farm to me?"

"Nothing," Cassy replied. "I appreciate you thinking about my future, but I believe I'm going to stay for a while. I like it here."

"Do you like it here because of the farm or do you like it here because of Lucas?" Colt locked his gaze with hers.

"What do you mean by that?" Cassy asked.

"You'd have to be blind to not see the sparks flying when you and Lucas are together." Colt laughed.

"Lucas and I are just friends. I don't know what you're talking about, sparks." Cassy didn't understand if Colt could see sparks when she and Lucas were together, what did he see when she looked at him?

"Right. Go ahead and play dumb. Even your grandfather mentioned it."

"He never said anything to me," Cassy replied. "Let's change the subject if you don't mind!" Cassy insisted.

"Whatever you say." Colt stood up, put his hat on and headed for the backdoor. "I have to go back to work."

"Have a great day, Colt." Cassy watched him wave and walk out the door.

"Sparks, huh? You have no idea about sparks. I'll show you sparks."

****

The service for James Conner was full. It seems as if everyone in town showed up to express their condolences. Cassy hadn't seen this many people at once since she'd arrived here. She was glad the service was over, but now came settling down on the farm without her grandfather around.

"Cassy." A voice came from behind her. "Wait a minute. I want to talk to you."

She watched as Lucas tried to make his way around the crowd towards her.

"Lucas. What's going on?"

"I wanted to talk to you for a minute. Do you have the time?" Lucas asked.

"Of course. What do you want to talk about?"

"I have to get back to work soon, but I wanted to see if you would like have dinner with me next week." Lucas paused for a minute. "I'm sorry Cassy. I wasn't thinking. I know this is a hard time for you. I can't believe I'm asking you out to dinner at your grandfather's funeral."

"It's all right, Lucas. I would like to have dinner with you." Cassy nodded.

"Why don't I call you in the next few days and we'll make arrangements?" Lucas smiled.

"That's sounds great. I'll look forward to it." She made her way around the room after Lucas left. She was lost without her grandfather. Thank goodness for Lucas and Colt.

****

Cassy was surprised by the knock on the front door.

"Who would come to the front door? Nobody ever comes to the front door." She put the dish towel down on the cabinet and headed to the living room.

"Ms. Cassandra Conner?"

Cassy didn't recognize the older gentleman wearing a dress shirt showing spots of sweat standing at the door. He was looking heated from the afternoon sun and a younger man dressed similar behind him was fanning himself with a manila folder.

"Yes. Can I help you?"

"I'm Detective Sloan and this is Detective Rogers." The older gentleman flipped open a small black case containing his badge. "May we come in?"

"Yes, of course." Cassy stepped aside and let the two men enter the living room. They both stopped right inside the door.

"What can I do for you?" Cassy moved in front of them.

"We would like to ask you some questions about your grandfather's death. Can we sit down?" Detective Sloan asked.

"I'm sorry. Where are my manners?" Cassy pointed to the couch and chair. "Please, have a seat. Can I get you something to drink? Some iced tea or cold water? You both look a little warm."

"Some water would be good," Detective Sloan replied.

"Same for me please," Detective Rogers said.

"I'll be right back." Cassy poured two glasses of water from the pitcher in the refrigerator and returned to the living room.

"What can I answer for you about my grandfather's death?" Cassy handed each of them a glass.

"We were called after the coroner received the results of the autopsy. We believe your grandfather's death wasn't from natural causes." Detective Sloan took a drink of water then placed the glass on the table in front of him.

"What do you mean?" Cassy asked. "I just assumed his heart gave out. It wasn't in the best of shape because of his diabetes."

"According to the Coroner's report his diabetes was the cause of his death, but we believe he had some help."

"What exactly are you getting at Detective Sloan?" Cassy shook her head. She was having a hard time processing what he was trying to say.

"We believe, whether by accident or on purpose, your grandfather took the wrong insulin. We need to find out exactly what happened that night so we can put this question to rest," Detective Sloan replied.

"You mean you think Grandpa either took the wrong insulin by accident or somebody switched his insulin?" Cassy sat up straight as she laughed. "I can't believe that. I was sitting right beside him when he took his shot after dinner. I helped him measure the dose and he even let me give him the shot. I've been practicing just in case."

"In case what?" Detective Rogers finally piped in.

"In case my grandfather got sick or was somehow incapable of giving himself his own shots. I needed to know how much he took, when, why. All the important information." Cassy explained.

"So, you knew what type of insulin he took, when and how much to give him?" Detective Rogers asked.

"Yes." Cassy nodded. "I was working with Grandpa and Lucas Harding. Lucas was teaching me how to count the carbohydrates Grandpa had eaten and how much insulin he took as a result. I learned he took Humalog after each meal because it was the quick acting insulin and before bed he would take Lantus which is the long acting insulin that kept his blood sugars down during the night."

"It sounds like you have quite a bit of knowledge on the subject. In fact, you would have enough knowledge you could switch your grandfather's insulin and cause him to go into a diabetic coma," Detective Sloan replied.

"That's crazy. I would never do that or even think of doing that!" Cassy exclaimed. "I really don't appreciate you insinuating I would do anything of the kind."

"The results of the Corner report show your grandfather slipped into a diabetic coma because the insulin he took. I understand from the logs at the EMT station, there've been several calls to this address because your grandfather had problems with his blood sugar being too low. Am I right?" Detective Sloan read from a notebook he pulled from the pocket of his shirt. "I can give you the dates if you would like."

"No, it's not necessary." Cassy remembered how familiar Lucas was with her grandfather and the house and how Colt explained they had to call for help before.

"Yes, my grandfather had one spell since I've come back to the farm. The first day I was here, he laid down to rest and his blood sugar went low. We had to call the paramedics. Luckily Lucas Harding was on duty. He's very familiar with my grandfather and his diabetes. Or I should say he was very familiar." Cassy paused for a minute. "The next time we called the paramedics was the morning my grandfather passed. Those are the only two times I've been here."

"Tell me exactly what happened the night your grandfather passed. Please don't leave anything out." Detective Rogers said.

"Okay. I'll do my best." Cassy took a breath before she began. "My grandfather and I ate breakfast. He took his shots while I cleaned up the kitchen. We took a ride around the farm. He wanted to show me some of the new projects. We ran into a neighbor when we drove down the road to see his newly remodeled house."

"You mean the Thompson?" Detective Rogers interrupted. "What do you think about that remodeling job? It's a good thing it was their son who was responsible or I'd have to shoot the designer." Detective Rogers laughed.

"Continue Ms. Conner. What happened after that?" Detective Sloan gave a disapproving look to Detective Rogers.

"After we left the Thompson's, we came home and had lunch. Grandfather was doing some work at the desk while I fixed him a sandwich. He ate then went and laid down for a little while. I cleaned up the lunch dishes. Colt came in looking for Grandpa. We talked for a few minutes and then he took a list and some money because he was going into town for supplies. Grandpa woke up and we had dinner. I helped him take his shot, he read some in the living room and I went outside to enjoy the evening. I came back in to go to bed. I poured Grandpa a glass of milk and put some cookies on a plate and he went to bed and so did I. I remember waking up to a noise."

"What noise was that?" Detective Sloan asked.

"It was Colt. He'd gotten home from town and was putting the supplies he bought in the kitchen. I returned to my room and went back to sleep. The next thing I knew it was morning. I was going to make breakfast and check on Grandpa. That's when I found him. Colt came in before and he was with me when we found him. He called 911 and you know everything after that."

"No one else was alone with you grandfather the day he died?" Detective Sloan asked.

"No. Grandfather and I were together most of the day. The only time I wasn't with him was after dinner when I went outside and then when I was in my room watching television."

"Could anyone else have come by to visit while you were in your room?" Detective Rogers asked.

"I would have heard if someone had come to visit. I don't believe so. The only other person who has free run of the house is Colt, and like I told you he was in town buying supplies. He didn't get home until after we had both gone to bed."

"Are you sure about when he returned home?" Detective Rogers asked.

"I woke up around one o'clock. That's when I heard the noise in the kitchen. I slipped down the hallway and Colt was in the kitchen putting supplies on the table. I assume he had just gotten home."

"Thanks, Ms. Conner, for your time." Detective's Sloan and Rogers both stood up at the same time as each handed Cassy a business card. "I'm sure we'll need to talk to you again. Please let us know if you leave town."

Cassy stood up and walked to the front door with the two detectives. She wasn't sure what else to say or if she should even say anything else, but she had to know.

"Do you think my grandfather was murdered?"

"We really don't want to speculate, Ms. Conner. The evidence will speak for itself if we give it time."

That line sounded like one some television detective would use. Cassy needed to find out what was going on. *Lucas*. He would tell her exactly what these two were digging for.

CHAPTER TWELVE

"Hello." Lucas answered his cell phone.

"Lucas, it's Cassy Conner. I hope I didn't catch you at a bad time."

"No, not at all."

"Good. I needed to ask you a question." Cassy continued. "I had two detectives visit me this afternoon. They were asking questions about the day my grandfather passed away. They told me they didn't think my grandfather died of natural causes."

"Really. What else did they say?" Lucas asked.

"They said he died by taking the wrong kind of insulin. They believe someone switched his insulin. Can you help me understand what they are talking about?"

"I'll answer your questions the best I can. I'm off work right now. Why I don't I come over and we can talk."

"Thank you, Lucas." Cassy needed his help her understand. How could anyone hurt her grandfather. They had to be wrong.

****

"Hi Cassy."

"Lucas. Thanks for coming over." Cassy stepped outside the door and waited for Lucas to walk up to the door.

"Sure, Cassy."

"Come in. It's cooler in the house. I made some tea or I have some beer. What can I get you?" Cassy asked.

"A glass of iced tea, please." Lucas at down at the kitchen table. "So, you mentioned the detectives paid you a visit. What exactly did they tell you again?"

"They think grandfather's death wasn't natural causes."

"What made them think that?" Lucas asked.

"The results of the autopsy showed Grandpa died from taking the wrong kind of insulin which made his blood sugar go low during. That sent him into a coma and he never came out of it." Cassy joined Lucas at the table placing two glasses of iced tea in front of them.

"I'm sure they did tests to show what was in his blood. So how do they think your grandfather received the wrong kind of insulin?"

"I was hoping you could tell me." Cassy leaned back in her chair crossing her legs at the knee. The way Lucas was looking at her suddenly made her uncomfortable. "I was learning how much he needed to take. but I don't know all the side effects of too much insulin versus too little or the wrong kinds versus the right."

"He could've been given or taken the wrong insulin in his nightly shot. If what they're saying is right, they probably think someone switched his fast acting with his long acting insulin. That would make his blood sugar go down very fast and put him in a coma." Lucas explained.

"There was no one else around the day Grandfather died. Colt and I were the only two people. Colt left in the afternoon to go into town. He didn't get back until after midnight." Cassy uncrossed her legs and scooted up to the table.

"That only leaves you." Lucas' tone and expression gave her a chill.

"I could never do anything like they're saying. I loved my grandfather. I could've never even let a thought like that enter my head." Tears began to roll down her checks.

Lucas reached up and wiped one away. "I'm sure this will all be straightened out. The detectives will figure out what happened that night and everything will be all right."

"You think so?"

"I'm sure of it." Lucas smiled. "We might have to give them some help, but they'll figure it out."

"What do you mean? Give them some help." Cassy's eyebrows raised.

"I'm not quite sure yet," Lucas replied. "I'll let you know when I figure it out."

Cassy didn't like the look on Lucas' face. She wasn't comfortable with him here alone. Her body was covered with goose bumps. "Thanks for coming over Lucas. I don't know what I would've done if you hadn't come over." Cassy stood up and waited for Lucas to stand.

"I'm glad I could help."

"I'll walk you out to your truck." Cassy started out the back door with Lucas following. *I wish Colt was here.*

CHAPTER THIRTEEN

Colt stood back inside the dark of the barn as he watched Lucas walk out the back door of the door with Cassy following behind him.

"Well, well. Isn't that cozy? Old man Conner isn't even warm in his grave and she's entertaining gentlemen."

He watched Lucas climb in his truck and drive off. Cassy waved as he drove away and then walked back in the house.

"I guess it's about time Cassy and I had a talk. First the detectives, now Lucas. I better find out exactly what's going on." He put away the tools he was working with in the barn and headed towards the house.

He could see Cassy in the kitchen. Making some noise walking up to the house so he wouldn't scare her, he walked in the door.

"Hi Cassy." Colt took his hat off and hung it from the back of the chair. "Was that Lucas I saw leaving?"

"Yes, it was," Cassy replied. "I'm going to make myself a sandwich for dinner. Would you like something? I'll be happy to leave everything out."

"Sure. I'll make myself something since everything is out." Colt walked over to the sink and washed his hands.

"So, what did Lucas have to say? Anything important. He didn't want to stay for dinner?" Colt asked.

"Not much. He had to get back because he works a shift tonight. He was talking to me about the night grandfather passed." Cassy placed her sandwich plate down on the table and filled a glass with tea. "Did I tell you I had a visit from a couple of detectives?"

"No, you didn't. What did they want?"

Colt kept his back to Cassy so she couldn't see his reaction.

"They had some questions about grandfather's death."

"What kind of questions?" Colt finished making his sandwich and sat down at the table with Cassy.

"According to the Coroner's report Grandpa didn't die of natural causes."

"No way. How do they know that? What did they say he died of?" Colt asked.

"They seem to think he had some help. He had too much fast-acting insulin in his blood stream."

"So exactly what does that mean?" Colt took a bite of his sandwich while he listened.

"He accidently took the wrong insulin or..." Cassy paused.

"Or what?" Colt asked.

"Or someone switched his insulin before he took his nightly shot."

Colt sat up in his chair and looked at Cassy. "They told you that?"

"Yeah. They pretty much accused me of killing my grandfather."

"That's crazy." Colt placed his sandwich down on his plate.

"They don't seem to think so. I was the only one with him most of the day. You were in town buying supplies and didn't get home until after midnight."

"How do you know what time I got home?" Colt was surprised by Cassy's remark.

"I woke up when you were putting the supplies in the kitchen. I assumed you were just getting home."

"Oh, yes. Yes, I was just getting home. I didn't think I woke anyone. I'm sorry about that," Colt replied.

"Anyway, I guess I'm the only logical person." Cassy took a bite of her sandwich.

"Did the detectives say what they're going to do about this?" Colt linked his fingers in front of him.

"Not really. They just said they're still looking into the evidence and they would get back to me." Cassy took a drink of her tea.

"Wow, I've never known anyone accused of murder. You don't look the type." Colt shook his head.

"Not funny Colt. Knock it off." Cassy glared at Colt. She grabbed her plate and rinsed it off and placed it in the sink.

"I'm sorry, Cassy. I didn't mean to upset you. I understand this has to be hard for you knowing they might think you had something to do with your grandfather's death. Your grandfather's death was hard enough. I can't imagine adding this to it." Colt walked over to the sink and put his hand on her arms. "I'm here for you if you need me. Just let me know what you need. To talk, to run an errand, whatever." He could feel Cassy's body tensed up as his closeness became apparent to her.

"I'll be fine Colt. Don't worry about me."

"I am worried about you. You're upset and I don't know what to do to help." Colt moved closer.

"Thanks Colt. I don't want you to worry about me. I just need you to be around to talk to and help with the farm. It's been a lot this past week."

He could see the tears begin to fall down her cheeks. "I'm here to do whatever you need me to do. Well at least I have you as an alibi."

"What are you talking about?" Cassy pulled away from his grip as she turned to face him. "Your alibi?"

"Yeah. You know a person who can vouch for were you were and all that stuff."

"You were in town buying supplies."

"Exactly. There's no way I could've had anything to do with your grandfather's death. I was in town buying supplies." Colt smiled. "You're my alibi and a beautiful one at that."

Colt leaned in and kissed her. The kiss didn't last long as Cassy pushed him away.

"What are you doing?"

"Kissing you. Haven't you ever been kissed before?" Colt held on tight to her arms.

"Let me go Colt. That was totally out of line!" Cassy exclaimed.

"Are you sure? I gave it my best shot."

Cassy pulled her arms free of his grip and moved away. "Why don't you leave?" Cassy pointed at the back door.

"Come on Cassy. Don't be mad. I thought it might take your mind off your grandfather. How long's it been since you had a man kiss you?" Colt began to move toward her, but stopped in his tracks when he felt the sting of her hand across his face.

"I said leave. Now!" The expression on Cassy's face must have told him everything he needed to know.

"Sure. I'll leave. Let me know if you change your mind."

"Don't worry, I won't."

Colt picked up his cowboy hat off the back of the chair, combed his fingers through his hair then put his hat on his head. "You know where to find me."

CHAPTER FOURTEEN

Cassy couldn't believe what just happened. How could he have thought she enjoyed kissing him? What did she do to make him think it would be all right? They were talking about her grandfather's death and then he kissed her.

First it was the uncomfortable feeling she got when Lucas was looking at her and now Colt trying to kiss her.

What the hell? Cassy headed upstairs. She needed to take a bath, anything to get the thought of Colt out of her head and Lucas right along with him.

She was just as disgusted with herself as much as she was with Colt. He was trying to comfort her in his own way and she had to admit, she actually did enjoy his kiss. It had been a long time since she had been kissed by a man. He was right and the thought made her have a knot it the pit of her stomach.

"Don't go there Cassy." She grumbled as she grabbed her bathrobe and started the water in the bathtub. This time she was locking the bathroom door and shutting the world out.

Sliding down into the bubbles of the bathtub, she closed her eyes and Colt was there. His mouth pressed against her. She could feel his firm body and smell his scent as plain now as when it happened. The sensation was over taking her. She didn't want to like the feeling but she knew she wanted it to happen again.

Cassy slipped on a nightgown and her robe and headed downstairs for a glass of milk before she turned in for the night. Her body was finally making the adjustment her internal alarm had made of getting up early and going to bed after the evening news. She didn't think her life would ever be routine like it was now.

She poured a glass of milk and walked outside. The sky was perfectly clear and stars were visible from every piece of the sky. She sat down in the swing along the side of the house enjoying the cool breeze of the evening.

"I'm sorry about earlier." Colt's voice came from out of the darkness. She caught a glimpse of his outline as he came closer to her. She was still mad at him but she enjoyed what she saw. The closer he moved towards her, the stronger she could feel her body react. She caught the smell of musk. He must've just showered and shaved. Not only did he have a masculine air about him, but the scent of him made her blood pulse through her body at a rapid speed.

"I hope I didn't upset you. I asked you how long it had been since a man kissed you. I should have told you it's been a long time since I kissed a woman."

"Let's forget about it, Colt." Cassy took a sip of her milk. "I'm sorry I got so upset." She slid over on the swing giving him enough room to sit down beside her. "You were right by the way."

"Right about what?"

Colt put his arm across the back of the swing making heat flow deep through her body. She wanted him to touch her, to take her upstairs and make love to her, but Cassy knew she had to be careful what she shared with Colt. The idea of him was strong in Cassy and she knew in the right situation she was lost.

"It's been a long time since I was kissed by a man." Cassy looked down and fidgeted with a string on her robe. "But, that didn't make it all right for you to kiss me."

"I'll never figure you women out." Colt sighed.

"We aren't that difficult, Colt. You guys just make it harder than it has to be."

"Will you could give me a crash course?" Colt asked.

"Just treat us like you want to be treated. If you're nice and respectful, we respond." Cassy looked at him thinking how much she wanted him to try and kiss her again.

"What about kissing you wasn't nice or respectful? I was using my best moves." Colt laughed.

"Those were your best moves?" Cassy laughed. "You and I have a lot of work to do."

"What if we start right now?"

Cassy was overwhelmed by his scent and feel as he pulled her close to him, kissing her. At first, softly touching his lips on hers then covering her mouth completely with his, pressing his moist hot lips on hers. He was wonderful and his breath was warm and intoxicating. The time Cassy couldn't push away. She couldn't breathe. It was as if his kiss was taking the life out of her and replacing it with a sensuous, relaxing flow of warmth over her entire body. She melted into him.

"How was that?"

Against her wishes Colt pulled his lips away from hers bringing her back to reality. She could hear her heart beating in her chest. She took a few seconds to catch her breath.

"Well, let's see. If I was going to rate that kiss versus the one earlier I would say this one was an eight."

"Just an eight?" Colt pulled her closer to him leaving no room between them, kissing her with a passion she'd never felt before. His hands caressed her body making himself familiar with the curves of her body.

"Colt." Cassy managed to pull herself away and take a breath. "I think we need to stop right here."

"But Cassy, I know you're enjoying this as much as I am."

"I'm not saying I'm not enjoying it. We have to work together Colt. I don't think this is a good idea." Cassy adjusted her robe and stood up from the swing. Colt stood up next to her. "Good night Colt. I'll see you tomorrow."

"Good night Cassy." Colt gave her a peck on the cheek and patted her firm buttocks with his hand. "You know where to find me if you change your mind." Cassy watched as he walked away back to the barn. Knowing where to find him could be a bad, bad thing for her.

CHAPTER FIFTEEN

Rinsing her face in the bathroom sink, Cassy looked at her reflection in the mirror. There were dark circles under her eyes even though she had slept in a little longer than usual. Getting to sleep last night was hard when she couldn't stop thinking about Colt's kisses. After managing to drift off to sleep, he invaded her dreams. She tossed and turned all night.

"What are you getting yourself into?"

Cassy didn't have a chance to go any further with her thoughts because they were interrupted by her cell phone ringing.

"Hello."

"Cassy, it's Lucas Harding."

"Good morning Lucas. How are you?"

"Listen Cassy, I was wondering if you could meet me in town this morning? I want to talk to you about our conversation yesterday. I think I might have some information that could help out."

"Sure, I can meet you. When and where?"

"Can you drive into town? How about at the café in about an hour? Would that work for you?"

"I'll meet you there." Cassy started to end the call when she heard Lucas' voice.

"And Cassy."

"Yes."

"Would you come alone? I don't want Colt to know what you are up to."

"Why?" Cassy felt strange about his request and now about this meeting. What was it exactly Lucas wanted to tell her.

"I'll explain when you get here. See you soon."

Cassy ended the call and put her cell phone down on the night stand. "What am I going to tell Colt? He's going to want to know why I'm going into town."

Cassy slipped on a pair of jeans, pulled her hair back and put on a light touch of makeup to cover the dark circles. She glanced at the clock, grabbed her purse and headed for the back door.

"Good morning Sunshine."

Cassy heard Colt's voice coming from the barn.

"Going somewhere?" Cassy turned to catch a glimpse of Colt throwing bales of hay into the back of his truck.

"Good morning, Colt." She threw her purse in the front seat of the truck. "I've got to go into town. I just remembered I have an appointment I'm going to be late for."

"Do you need me to go with you? I can make it into town faster than anyone in the county."

"I don't think you want to go with me for this appointment." She hated lying to him but she couldn't tell him the truth.

"Why?" Colt walked out the barn pushing his cowboy hat up on his forehead with his gloved finger.

"Let's just say it's a woman thing. I'll see you when I get back."

"Then why don't I plan on us having dinner together?"

Colt moved closer to her and kissed her on the cheek. He was so damn sexy. Hot, sweaty and gorgeous.

"Sure. That sounds great. I'll see you when I get back." Cassy hoped the tone of her voice let him know she was looking forward to it.

"Drive safe." Colt waved as she headed down the drive.

Cassy began to mumble. "That was close." She knew she would have to make sure and thank Lucas for putting her in that awkward position. She wished she knew what this was all about."

****

Cassy pulled into an empty parking spot outside the café. Lucas was standing by the door waiting for her.

"Cassy." He waved as she climbed out of the truck.

"Hi, Lucas. How are you?"

"Okay." He opened the door to the café motioning for Cassy to enter first. "Let's go in and sit down."

"What's going on Lucas? You sounded like whatever you need to tell me is really important." Cassy followed him to a table and sat down across from him

"I've been asking around about the day your grandfather passed. You told me Colt was in town that afternoon and didn't get home until after midnight."

"Yes. Why?"

"According to some people around town, Colt headed back to the farm early in the evening. That would've put him home long before your grandfather turned in for the night."

"Ok. So, if he left town early evening. What does that mean?" Cassy wasn't sure what Lucas was trying to say.

"You said there was no one else around who had access to our grandfather except you. That's not true. Colt was there. If someone switched your grandfather's insulin and it wasn't you, that only leaves…"

"Colt." Cassy interrupted. She couldn't believe what she was hearing. "Why would he switch Grandpa's insulin?"

"I don't know. But we can keep digging." Lucas offered.

"I don't think we have to." Cassy just remember how funny Colt acted when she showed him the notebook her grandfather was looking at. "Are you off for the afternoon? I would like you to come with me somewhere. I want you to be there as a witness."

"Sure. First, let's eat something, I'm starving. Then we can go."

"Ok." Cassy agreed, but she knew she wasn't going to be able to eat much. Hearing what she just heard from Lucas made her sick to her stomach. Why did Colt lie to her?

****

Lucas jumped in the passenger side of the truck as Cassy started the engine. "Where are we going?"

"To the Thompson's."

"Why are you going there? I really hate looking at that house." Lucas laughed. "What a waste of good money."

"I'm not sure, but there's something I need to ask Mr. Thompson and I want you to be my witness."

The rest of the ride was in silence. Cassy needed to clear her head before she talked to Mr. Thompson or she could screw this up totally. She understood now why her grandfather was going through the notebook in his desk after they had returned that day. He was checking up on Colt. The feeling of panic filled up her entire body.

Cassy pulled into the drive way of the Thompson house. She opened the door and climbed out of the car with Lucas right behind her.

"Cassy, wait!" Lucas was out of breath as he tried to catch up to her.

"Are you coming or not Lucas?" Cassy kept going.

"I guess I'm coming."

Cassy was met at the door by Mr. Thompson. "Cassandra Conner. I didn't expect you to be back so soon. How are you doing since your grandfather's passing? Is there anything we can do for you?"

"I need to ask you a question Mr. Thompson." Cassy tried to sort in her mind how she was going to ask a question she needed an answer to.

"Sure Cassandra. What is it?"

"Remember the day my grandfather and I stopped by you two were talking about the stud service you paid for?" Cassy asked.

"Sure. I remember." Mr. Thomson nodded his head.

"How much did you say you paid for the service?" Cassy watched as he raised his head and rubbed his chin.

"Fifty thousand."

"Thank you, Mr. Thompson. You've been a lot of help." Cassy climbed back into the truck and started the engine. Lucas barely made it in the truck before she took off.

"Why are you in such a hurry?" Lucas was still out of breath from trying to keep up with her.

"I think I know what happened. When Grandpa and I stopped at the Thompson's that day, Mr. Thompson made the comment about the stud fee. When we got home, Grandpa checked the notebook in his desk. After he went to sleep I took a look at the notebook, but I didn't put two and two together. Now I know what I'm looking for."

"What?" Lucas asked.

"I have to make sure before I say. I'll take you back to your car and you can either meet me back at the ranch or not. It's your choice."

"Why don't we just go to the ranch together now?" Lucas asked.

"I don't want Colt to get suspicious. If you come home with me now, he'll know I lied to him. It'll blow everything." Cassy did want to take the time to make Lucas understand.

"I don't know what you are talking about, but I'll trust you," Lucas replied.

"I'll let you know if I need you to do anything, but right now I have to do this by myself." Cassy explained. She couldn't wait to get back to the ranch and Colt.

CHAPTER SIXTEEN

Cassy parked next to the house. As she climbed out of the truck, she looked to see if Colt was in the barn. She didn't see him anywhere as she headed inside the house.

"So how did the Doctor's appointment go?"

Cassy found Colt standing in the kitchen as she walked in the backdoor.

"I guess fine." Cassy hoped he didn't catch the surprised look on her face. "I really hate that type of appointment, but there's not much I can do. I have to go."

"Everything checked out all right?" Colt laughed moving his fingers to make air quotes.

"Funny." Cassy smiled. "I think everything checked out fine. Thanks for asking."

"Good. I thought we could have steaks for dinner tonight, maybe a salad and some fresh ears of corn."

"That sounds great. Would you mind if I took a quick bath first and then I'll come back down and help you?" Cassy asked.

"You have plenty of time. Go ahead. I've got to go check the herd. I'll be back soon." Colt took his hat off the chair and walked out the back door.

She knew if she didn't calm down she was going to make him suspicious. Cassy knew she had to keep her cool if she was going to get Colt to give her the information she needed. She needed to find out what exactly was going on and if he lied to her. She would've never thought it was possible, but now she wasn't sure. She grabbed her purse, the notebook from her grandfather desk and headed upstairs.

****

After she dried off, Cassy slipped on a pair of Capri slacks and a sleeveless blouse and headed to the kitchen. Placing the notebook back in the desk where she found it, she thought she heard Colt come back in the house.

"Colt?" She yelled as she walked towards the kitchen.

"Hi." He walked over and gave her a kiss on the cheek. "How was your bath?"

"It was refreshing. How was the herd?"

"They're all present and accounted for. I shucked the ears of corn and put them in some water on the stove. All we have to do is turn the fire on. The steaks are seasoned on the platter in the fridge. We can make the salad while the steaks are cooking."

"That works for me. I'll make the salad then come out and keep you company while the steaks cook." Cassy took a deep breath and reminded herself what she needed to know.

"I'm going to enjoy a beer before we start dinner. It's a hot one out there today." Colt held up the beer in his hand and then headed outside.

Cassy took a beer from the refrigerator, opened it then went outside to join Colt. "I'm ready for dinner anytime you want to start the grill."

"It's already started, if you want to go get the steaks out of the fridge. I was just waiting for you to say you were hungry." Colt offered.

"I'll grab you another beer and the steaks and be right back."

"Sounds good." Colt stood from the swing and handed Cassy his empty bottle. "Would you get rid of that for me?"

"Sure. I'll be right back." Cassy walked into the house put the empty bottle in the trash. She took the lettuce, cucumber and tomatoes out of the refrigerator and placed them on the counter. She turned the fire on under the corn, took out the steaks, another beer and headed back outside. "Here you go."

"Thanks." Colt took the beer and steaks from her and placed them on the table beside the grill.

"I didn't get a chance to eat lunch while I was in town because of my appointment so I'm starving." Cassy felt funny lying to Colt, but she couldn't tell him she didn't eat much lunch because her stomach felt funny after she Lucas told her Colt was lying to her. Who does she believe?

"Which Doctor did you go see? Old Doctor Smith? I bet he loves having beautiful young women like you come in for their appointments."

"No. I didn't see Doctor Smith." Cassy quickly tried to think of something to say not to give herself away. "I don't remember the Doctor's name. He was one of the newer Doctor's in town." Cassy hoped she covered well enough Colt wouldn't ask her anymore questions. It was her night to find out information not his.

****

"Dinner was good. Thank you." Cassy began picking up their plates from the table and took them to the sink.

"Your welcome. Let me help you." Colt picked up the rest of the dishes and carried them to the sink. "Why don't you let me take care of those?"

"Are you sure? I don't mind washing the dishes since you cooked dinner."

"How about if I wash and you dry?" Colt smiled as he squeezed his way in front of the sink.

"That sounds fair." Cassy picked up the dish towel and leaned against the cabinet watching Colt as he ran water in the sink and added the dish soap.

"I think if I still live here when I start a family, I'm going to have to remodel the kitchen and put in a dishwasher."

"You mean give up all the fun of hand washing the dishes? That's just crazy talk." Colt smiled sending a now familiar chill down Cassy's body all the way to her toes.

"It might be crazy talk to you, but not me. I can't believe my grandmother lived all these years without some of the modern conveniences we all take for granted."

"I guess she was happy with what she had." Colt handed her the first washed and rinsed plate.

"I believe she was. I don't remember my grandmother ever being unhappy. All my memories of her are good ones. She was always smiling or laughing." Memories of her grandmother always made Cassy smile. She could almost feel the love flowing through her body like she did when her grandmother would give her a huge hug. She missed those hugs.

"So, you want a family huh?" Colt asked.

"Yes. Some day. Don't you?"

"I guess so. I haven't really thought about it. It wouldn't be bad having a little Colt running around."

Cassy couldn't let the twinkle she saw in the corner of his eye distract her from what she really needed to know. She needed to find out if he was in town the night her grandfather died or if he came back early like Lucas said.

"You know if you do find a woman and settle down, she probably isn't going to like you going into town and staying out most of the night like you did the other night." Cassy hoped heading down this line of conversation would give her the chance to find out more about the night her grandfather died.

"I think that's probably the reason I haven't settled down or given much thought to kids. I'm still having a good time and I'm not ready to give that up." Colt handed her another plate.

"What exactly do you find to do in town? I never could figure that out. This is such a small town there can't be much to keep you busy after ten o'clock. You can only go line dancing a few times before it gets boring." Cassy took another plate from Colt, taking her time drying off the water and then putting it down on the cabinet as she waited for him to answer her question.

"I usually have dinner and a few cups of coffee at the café. Then head down to the tavern to shoot some pool and catch up with all the guys. By that time, it's after midnight and the drive back makes it an early morning. Line dancing is only once a month or so. It's never boring."

"Is that pretty much what you did the other night when you were in town?"

"Yep. I usually don't change my routine up much."

"So, that's why you woke me that night. You were just getting home from town." Cassy waited for him to answer because this was his chance to tell her the truth or lie.

"I'm sorry about waking you up. That's right. I was just getting back to the ranch and I remembered your supplies. Why are you asking me so many questions?"

He couldn't even look at her. Cassy watched his expression and he didn't even skip a beat or change his expression at all. He was good. Good at telling lies.

"No reason." Cassy paused for a minute. "You promised me a raincheck for a night of dancing. I just wondered what I was getting myself into."

Finishing up the dishes Cassy put them away in the cabinets. There wasn't much said between the two of them after Colt lied without even blinking an eye. She wasn't sure what to do now. This was going to be a problem which required some thought. She felt colt's arms slip around her waist.

"How about we go outside and enjoy the evening?" He whispered in her ear.

"You know what Colt, after my Doctors appointment today, I'm tired. I'm going to take some aspirin and go to bed. How about a rain check?" Cassy laid the dishtowel down on the cabinet.

"Are you sure?"

Cassy turned around and looked in his eyes knowing she was about to tell the biggest lie ever. "Positive."

"I was looking forward to us spending some time together tonight." He was making it extremely difficult to say no. His eyes were burning holes of desire straight through to her soul. She could see the disappointment showing on his face.

"I guess we can try again tomorrow night." The disappointment rang in his voice.

"Tomorrow night will be better." Cassy smiled as Colt pulled her closer and kissed her. It didn't feel the same as it did yesterday. If it was possible, it was more intense. Pleasure was surging through every part of her body. His kisses took her breath away. It was more than just a kiss. It was a kiss from the lips of someone she didn't know if she could trust and she was going to have to find out if he had something to do with her grandfather's death.

CHAPTER SEVENTEEN

"Detective Sloan, please." Cassy twirled the business card in her hand as she waited for him to come to the phone. She knew this was something she wouldn't be able to find the answers to alone. *I hope I'm doing the right thing.*

"This is Detective Sloan. How can I help you?"

"This is Cassy Conner. I was wondering if I could talk to you."

"Sure Ms. Conner. What can I do for you?"

"I'd really like to talk in person. Would it be possible for you to make a trip out to the farm?"

"I think I could manage that, Ms. Conner. How about if I come out this afternoon? Say around two."

"I'll be here. Thank you, Detective Sloan." Cassy ended the phone call.

Cassy tried to imagine what Colt was going to do when Detective Sloan shows up again. She would have to wait and see. The sooner this was over and they got to the truth, the better.

****

Cassy was standing by the front door when the Detective's car pulled in the driveway. She waited for them to walk up to the front door before she opened it to let them in.

"Detective Sloan. Detective Rogers, thank you for coming out."

"Ms. Conner. You sounded like it was important. Why don't we sit down and you tell me what you think I need to know?"

Cassy sat in the chair as the detectives took a seat on the couch.

"What I wanted to talk to you about was some information I found out this week. I know you're investigating what happened to my grandfather and I think the information I have will help you out." Cassy was having a hard time sitting still. She wanted this to be over.

"Why don't you take your time and tell us what this information is Ms. Conner?" Detective Sloan took out a note pad from his jacket pocket.

"The last time you were here I called Lucas Harding after you left. I needed to talk to someone about what we'd discussed and Lucas was the perfect person. He knew my grandfather illness well because he was one of the paramedics to answer the calls when he had problems and he had worked with my grandfather helping him learn how to control his diabetes."

"Was Mr. Harding helpful when you talked to him?" Detective Sloan asked.

"Yes. He explained to me what you meant by my grandfather having too much insulin in his blood stream and how that could have happened. We came to the same conclusion you had and that was his insulin had to have been switched." Cassy waited for Detective Sloan's reaction.

"Is this the information you have to share with me Ms. Conner? If so, you're wasting my time repeating what I told you."

"No, Detective Sloan. I apologize for not getting to the point sooner. The information I have to share with you is if you remember when I told you Colt Matthews had left for town late in the afternoon and didn't get back until early morning?"

"Yes, I do remember."

"Well, Lucas told me he was talking to some people in town and found out Colt wasn't in town all night. He left town early in the evening and had plenty of time to make it back to the farm before my grandfather turned in that night. Colt was familiar with my grandfather illness. He knew about the insulin, but the most important piece of information to remember was me telling you I saw my grandfather going through his books at the desk?" Cassy pointed to the desk where the books were located.

"Yes, I remember," Detective Sloan replied.

"Well, I checked with Mr. Thompson again asking him what he paid for the stud fee he was charged for my grandfather's prize bull. Mr. Thompson told me he paid fifty thousand dollars for the stud fee. My grandfather's books show he only charged Mr. Thompson forty thousand for the fee. Here look at this." Cassy picked up the notebook from the table where she'd placed it then handed it to Detective Sloan. "This is the notebook Grandpa kept his records of customers, when they purchased, how much he charged and if the insemination worked."

"This is all well and good, Ms. Conner, but I don't understand what you are getting at."

"I'm trying to tell you I think Colt Matthews was skimming from my grandfather by increasing stud fees to his customers and keeping the extra money for himself." Cassy watched both of the detective's expressions. They showed no change.

"That's a pretty big accusation, Ms. Conner. Are you sure about that?"

"You can check the bank deposits and ask my grandfather's customers. I'll be happy to give you a list of customers and what they paid."

"And if we find out Colt was skimming money like you think, then what?" Detective Rogers asked.

"What do you mean then what?" Cassy asked. "Colt might have been trying to hide this information. He might have switched my grandfather's insulin. He could be the reason my grandfather is dead. I don't want to believe it, but it's a possibility."

"I tell you what, Ms. Conner, we'll do some asking around and see if the information you've given us is correct and we'll let you know what we find."

Cassy stood up with the detectives and walked with them to the door.

"I'll be waiting to hear from you, Detective Sloan. Detective Rogers. Please let me know what you find out."

"We will, Ms. Conner. I would suggest you don't say anything to Colt Matthews about what you told us," Detective Sloan said.

"Sure. Do you think I'm in danger staying here with Colt in the bunkhouse?" Cassy asked.

"Do you have someone who can stay with you?" Detective Rogers asked.

"No. No one I can think of right now."

"My suggestion would be to not say anything to Mr. Matthews about our conversation. We'll check out what you told us as soon as we can." Detective Sloan stepped out the front door with Detective Rogers Close behind. "Thank you for your time, Ms. Conner."

Cassy watched as they drove off. "What now?"

"Who was that?" Colt asked as he walked in the back door.

"You mean driving off?" Cassy asked.

"Yeah. It looked like one of those detectives that were here a few days ago."

Cassy watched as he took his hat off and hung it on the back of the chair. He ran his fingers through his hair and it fell perfectly back into place. He was so gorgeous. What she was thinking couldn't be true. How could he have hurt her grandfather?

"It was. Detective Sloan and Detective Rogers."

"What were they doing here again?"

They were updating me on the findings of the Corner autopsy. They don't know for sure what happened to Grandpa so they're calling the case an accident. They're saying Grandpa took the wrong insulin by mistake and they might be closing the case."

"How does that make you feel?" Colt asked.

"I'm not sure. I guess it's good to know there isn't someone out there who could do that kind of thing and get away with it." Cassy started walking towards the kitchen. "I'm going to make some soup and a sandwich for dinner. Would you like something?"

"How about you?" Colt put his arms out and pulled her to him as she tried to pass by.

"You know Colt it seems like I'm always pushing you away." Cassy couldn't help but wonder how this man who made her body burn with desire could be guilty of killing her grandfather. "I'm sorry, but talking about my grandfather's death brings back a lot of unhappy memories. It's just not a good time."

"I can understand that. Let's make a sandwich and some soup then?" Colt walked into the kitchen took two bowls and plates out of the cabinets.

"Sounds good." Cassy attempted a smile.

They both ate their dinner in silence. Cassy couldn't get past the fact Colt had lied to her about the night her grandfather died. Her head was telling her she couldn't trust him and she should be afraid of what he could do, but her body and heart was telling her to keep an open mind until the truth was found out. If he was going to do anything to her, he more than had his chance.

Nothing is ever as it seems. She wasn't sure whether to listen to her head or her heart.

****

Colt was glad he got up early to do his daily inspection of the farm. It was going to be a miserably hot day. A dip in the farm pond might be in order today. Maybe he could talk Cassy into joining him. He took the saddle off the horse and led her to the stall. He threw the saddle over the railing and headed back to the stall to brush down the horse.

"Colt Matthews?" Detective Sloan and Detective Rogers appear in the doorway of the barn.

"Yes. I'm Colt Matthews."

"I'm Detective Sloan and this is Detective Rogers." He flipped open the cases contained his badge giving Colt a chance to look closely. "We would like you to come down to the station with us. We would like to ask you a few questions."

"About what?" Colt asked.

"About the night James Conner was murdered."

"Murdered?" Colt was confused about what he was saying. "Cassy told me you were thinking of closing the case and ruling it an accident."

"Well, in light of some new evidence we're keeping it open," Detective Sloan replied. "As I said before, we would like you to come with us so we can ask you some questions."

"You have to take me down to the station for that? I can tell you what you want to know right here and then you can be on your way." Colt continued brushing down his horse.

"You see, Mr. Matthews, we also want to talk to you about how you skimmed money from James Conner." Detective Sloan locked gaze with him.

"What are you talking about?" Colt asked. "I haven't skimmed money from anyone."

"If you come peacefully we won't use handcuffs, but if you resist we'll change the rules." Detective Sloan stood on one side of Colt and Detective Rogers on the other. They walked him slowly towards their car, each one keeping a grip on Colt's arms. Opening the door, they placed him in the back seat.

All Colt could think about right now was Cassy. She didn't know where he was going and he probably wouldn't get a chance to tell her. What if they arrested him and threw him in jail?

"How am I going to explain this to her?"

****

Cassy watched as the Detectives drove out the driveway with Colt in the backseat. "What have I done?"

Cassy sat down at the kitchen table and cried. She wasn't sure what to feel. Her emotions were all jumbled. She missed her grandfather. If someone helped him die she wanted that person to pay, but she didn't want it to be Colt. All the evidence they had pointed to him, but she didn't want to believe it. She was sure she could feel her heart breaking.

CHAPTER EIGHTTEEN

"We understand you were in town the night James Conner died. Is that correct?" Detective Sloan asked.

"Yes, it's correct," Colt replied.

"Can you tell us exactly what you did that night? Why you were in town."

"I'd be happy to tell you why I was in town and what I did that night." Colt took a deep breath to try and keep his composure. "I went into town to get some supplies. I'd gotten a list and some money from Cassy. I had dinner at the café and a few cups of coffee then I headed for the tavern to play a few games of pool."

"What did you do after that? Surely what you've told us wouldn't have taken you all night. We understand you didn't make it home until early the next morning." Detective Sloan made some notes on a pad of paper.

"I don't know what you've heard." Colt paused for a minute trying to be careful not to give them any information they could twist around on him.

"Why don't you tell us the truth so we know exactly what happened that night." Detective Sloan crossed his arms in front of him.

"Okay. I had a few beers at the tavern while I was playing pool. I started not feeling so well so I decided to head for home."

"What time was that?" Detective Rogers asked.

"It was around ten thirty, but I didn't make it all the way back to the farm." Colt paused for a minute.

"Why not?" Detective Sloan began making notes

"I had to pull my truck over about half way home because I got sick and I started feeling dizzy. I got out of the truck and threw up. I climbed back in the truck with the intention of driving the rest of the way home. I don't remember anything else. I must have passed out in the truck."

"Sounds like you had more than a few beers," Detective Rogers glanced at Colt with his eyebrows raised.

"I swear I only had a few beers. They've never affected me like that before. I wasn't sure what to think. When I came to, I drove to the farm and remembered I had supplies for Cassy. I took them out of the truck and took them in the house. I put them on the kitchen table and headed for the bunkhouse to get some sleep.

"Did you still feel sick when you woke up the next morning?" Detective Sloan asked.

"Not really. I remember feeling a little weak and having a hard time focusing, but it went away after I showered and had a cup of coffee."

"Who did you drink beer and play pool with that night?" Detective Sloan asked.

"Let's see. I remember a couple of farmhands from the Thompson farm. I played a game of pool with one of them. Oh, and Lucas Harding. He and I played a game and he bought a pitcher while we played." Colt thought back to that night and couldn't remember anyone else. "That was about it. It was shortly after that I started feeling funny and headed home."

"Lucas Harding's name seems to pop up a lot," Detective Sloan replied.

"It's a small town. It's not surprising. In his line of work, he knows a lot of people." Colt rubbed the back of his neck.

"We did some checking, Mr. Matthews, and found out what you've been doing with the fees the Conner farm has been receiving for stud services associated with a prize bull." Detective Sloan opened a folder he had laying on the table in front of him.

"What are you talking about?" Colt asked.

"We got a warrant to search through your bank records and we found out you were splitting off some of the fee and putting that money into a separate bank account."

Taking off his cowboy hat, Colt ran his fingers through his hair and put his hat back on his head. "So, you know about the money." Colt knew he had to be very careful what he admitted to.

"I think I would like to consult my lawyer before I answer any more questions." Colt could only hope Bo Perkins was available.

****

"Bo, Its Colt." He paused for a minute. "I need your help."

"Sure, Colt. What can I do?" Bo Perkins asked.

"I need you to come bail me out of jail." Colt tried to hold back his true feelings of anger and frustration.

"What? Why? What on earth have you done?" Bo Perkins snorted.

"Nothing." Colt snapped. "It's a long story, Bo. Just get all my paperwork together and get down here right away. Make sure you bring the file you have on the Conner farm."

"Sure. I'll be right there. I'd say don't go anywhere, but I don't have to worry about that." Bo laughed.

"Funny, Perkins." Colt hung up the phone.

"Okay I'm ready." He stood up from the chair and waited for the officer to escort him to his cell.

"Back in, Colt. I'll let you know when you lawyer gets here."

Colt sat down on the cot in the cell. "Let's hope he hurries."

****

"What your trying to tell me, Mr. Matthews, is you used your money to keep the Conner farm afloat until James Conner got well and back on his feet. The money you added to the prize bull stud fees above what James Conner wanted to charge was a way for you to make back the money you invested in the farm. Does that sound about right?" Detective Sloan repeated what Colt had told him.

"My client has provided you with all the information you need to prove his innocence. The files I provided you shows every deposit and charge Colt has taken care of," Bo Perkins replied. "I don't believe there's anything else you need or any reason why you don't let him go."

"The Judge isn't available to set bail and we need a chance to go over all the evidence you've presented to us." Detective Sloan shifted through the stack of papers. "I'm afraid until the judge is available to set bail or we can verify this information, your client is going to have to be a guest of ours."

"You mean to tell me I have to stay here?" Heat flowed through his body as Colt felt the frustration building stronger. "Bo, can't you do something. I've got responsibilities at the farm. Cassy is there by herself. I don't know if she even knows all that needs to be done."

"Why don't you make her a list and we'll get it to her." Detective Sloan suggested.

"That's big of you." Colt laughed. "Why don't you let me go show I can show her?"

"Sorry Colt. It's not happening."

Colt let out a deep sigh. "I gave it a shot. No one can say I didn't try."

****

"You have a visitor, Mr. Matthews." The deputy unlocked the cell door.

"Who is it?" Colt stayed stretched out on the cot in his cell with his arm across his eyes.

"Follow me." Colt stood and followed the deputy to a room with windows, a metal table and a few chairs. He stepped inside the room and sat down.

"I'll go get your guest." The deputy stepped out the door and disappeared down the hallway. When he reappeared, Cassy was with him. He unlocked the door and she walked inside the room.

"Colt." Cassy whispered as she looked at him sitting at the table.

"What are you doing here, Cassy?" The last thing he wanted was to have her see him like this. It was hard for him to look her in the eyes. He was surprised when she put her arms out to hug him which was quickly shut down by the deputy. He really needed a hug from her.

"Mr. Perkins came by and paid me a visit."

Colt watched as Cassy sat down in the chair across to him.

"He told me everything. I can't believe what you did for my grandfather."

"I didn't do anything anyone else wouldn't have done," Colt still couldn't meet her gaze.

"Yes, you did."

Colt could hear Cassy's voice breaking. "You did a lot. I don't know how I'm going to repay you."

Finally glancing up to look at her, Colt could see tears welling up and begin to fall from Cassy's eyes. He reached up and wiped them away. He wanted to kiss her and tell her how he felt, but he knew now wasn't the right time. He had never met another woman who grabbed his heart like she had. There was nothing he could do about it. The first day he saw Cassy Conner he knew he was in trouble.

"You don't have to repay me. I was only trying to help your grandfather. He had just lost his wife. Their son, you father, was dead and you were the only family. He didn't want me to call you because he wanted you to live your life and not be tied down to the farm. With everything he was going through, I couldn't tell him the farm was in financial trouble. Not on top of everything else. He had been good to me."

"Bo said you kept him liquid with your own money until things turned around."

Colt could tell she was attempting a smile while the tears still streamed down her cheeks. "Yeah. I did."

"Colt, that's a lot more than anyone else would have done. I can't believe you're sitting here in jail because you were being an angel in disguise. I'm so sorry things have turned out this way. I promise I'll sell the farm if I have to and get you back your money."

"You're not selling the farm!" Colt exclaimed. "I won't let you do that, not even to pay me back."

"Colt, I don't have the money to pay you back. The only way I would be able to get it would be to sell the farm."

"I don't want you to pay me back. Not right now. We'll work it out. Over time I'll get my money back. If we agree to keep the stud fees at the price I was charging, I'll be paid back in less than two years." Colt leaned forward against the table.

"I would be willing to do that, if you're willing to wait that long to be repaid." Cassy offered.

"I'd be willing to wait forever to be repaid if it meant I could stay at the farm with you."

"Colt."

"I mean it Cassy. You drive me crazy. All I can think about is you." Colt could see the surprise in her eyes. "We need to get you out of here. We have things to take care of back at the farm."

Cassy smile this time wasn't an attempt. It was real and Colt thought for sure he could feel his heart melt in his chest.

****

All Colt could think about was how he couldn't spend another night in this jail cell. Even if he did spend it dreaming of Cassy he wanted out of here. He wanted to be back at the ranch where he could hold her in his arms and feel her next to his.

"Time to go." Colt's thoughts were interrupted by the deputy unlocking the cell door.

"What's going on?" Colt stood from his cot.

"The charges have been dropped. You're free to go." He held the door open waiting for Colt to walk through.

"I hope you're serious because this is a sick joke if you're not." Colt hurried through the open door.

"We just need to process you and you can leave. Follow me this way."

Colt followed the deputy. He couldn't believe he would be back at the farm and with Cassy soon.

"Here's everything you had on you when we checked you in. Make sure you go through it and that you have everything." The deputy handed him the envelope.

Colt dumped the envelope out on the counter. "It looks like it all here. Now get me the hell out of here."

"We're almost done. You need to sign here and then you'll be free to go." The deputy handed him a pen.

"I wish I could say this has been a pleasure Gentlemen." Colt signed the piece of paper, picked up all his belongings off the counter and put them in his pocket. He walked through the door to the lobby.

"Can I give you a ride home?" Cassy's voice surprised him.

Colt knew this was too good to be true. He was going home and Cassy Conner was taking him there.

"I'd love a ride. I can't wait to get home." Colt put his arm around her waist and headed for the door. He wanted to make sure he wasn't dreaming and he wasn't going to give anyone a chance to wake him before he got what he wanted.

****

Pulling up to the house Colt jumped out of the truck not giving Cassy on opportunity to even put the truck in park. He ran around to the driver's side of the truck and waited for her to climb out.

"Why are you in such a hurry?" Cassy asked.

"If you had just spent the past two days in jail, I'd like to see how excited you would be to finally be home." Colt picked Cassy up and spun her around in a circle. "I've been thinking about nothing but you for the past day." He kissed her lightly. "First things first. I want to take a shower."

"Why don't you do that? I'll fix us a sandwich and some iced tea. I'll meet you in the kitchen."

"You've got a deal lady." Colt took off running for the bunkhouse. "I promise I'll smell a lot better when I get done. Don't go anywhere."

"I'll be right here when you get back." Cassy smiled.

Colt couldn't believe what was happening. His life was turning around in circles so fast he was dizzy. His mother had always told him he would know when he met the right woman to just give fate a chance. Right now, he was glad he listened.

CHAPTER NINETEEN

Cassy made two sandwiches and filled two glasses with iced tea. She placed them on the table next to the plates. She watched at the back door waiting for Colt to come out of the bunkhouse. She saw him walking toward the house his shirt unbuttoned, the tale blowing as the warm breeze caressed his body. His exposed chest glistened from the sun shining on his skin. She couldn't keep her eyes from noticing the beads of water flowing down a pleasure trail begging to be followed. Cassy couldn't wait until he got within her reach. She wanted to feel him not only next to her. She wanted to drink him in, every inch.

"I've been waiting." Cassy smiled as he opened the door.

"I've been waiting for you." Colt pulled her close and kissed her hard and deep. She wasn't letting him go.

"I made you a sandwich." Cassy managed to get a few words out after catching her breath. "I don't know about you, but I think I can wait to eat mine."

"Me too."

Cassy took Colt's hands leading him down the hallway to her bedroom. She ran her hands over his chest, her fingers delicately combing the tufts of hair, kissing his skin as she took in the scent of him. His shirt fell to the floor. She made her way down his chest and unbuckled his belt and unzipped his jeans. She wanted him now and from the bulge in his jeans, Cassy knew he felt the same. She helped him with the buttons on her blouse and shorts. Colt managed to quickly unfasten her bra and leave it and her panties lying on the bedroom floor.

She wanted to take everything slow and enjoy every inch of each other, but she couldn't fight the desire rushing through her body and have him inside of her.

Colt laid her gently on the bed lying on top of her kissing her neck and down her chest. He caressed each of her breasts, cupping them in his hands and massaging them as he ran his tongue gently around each nipple. They responded to his touch, becoming hard, the excitement making her body react.

Cassy's body arched with each moment of pleasure, pressing her moist, wet crotch against his erection, making him harder. She gasped as his lips made their way between her legs. She ran her fingers through his hair as he made her moan with ecstasy. She wanted more. She wanted him inside her. Colt began kissing her stomach, moving his way back up her body until he found her breasts, hard and aching for him.

She placed her hands on his hips and pulled him up where she could feel him pressing firm against her. Moving her hips, she gave him complete access to her. She felt him enter her slowly, then pulling back out slowly, sending her body into waves of pleasure. Cassy's body moved in perfect rhythm with Colt until they both reached a moment of climax together.

Cassy moaned with pleasure begging Colt not to stop as she felt another wave come over her body. Colt didn't deny her anything. They both collapsed in exhaustion trying to catch their breath. Nothing was said. There were no words to follow what just happened. They told the other what they felt for each other with their bodies.

****

Cassy woke to sunrise shining through her bedroom window, birds chirping and an empty bed. She slipped on her bathrobe and headed down the hallway. There was a intoxicating fragrance coming from the kitchen. If she wasn't mistaken, she thought she heard someone singing along to the radio. Walking into the kitchen she caught a glimpse of Colt busy by the stove.

"You have a nice voice and something smells wonderful."

"Well, look who's awake." Colt smiled.

"What are you making?" She walked up behind Colt sliding her arms around his waist.

"I'm making you some bacon and eggs. I thought you might be hungry since we didn't get a chance to eat the sandwiches you made."

"That's why I'm starving." Cassy took two glasses out of the cabinet and pour each of them a glass of milk. "How long have you been awake?"

"For about an hour," Colt replied. "I watched you sleep for a little while then I slipped out of bed to come make us something to eat. I hope you don't mind, but I tossed the sandwiches we didn't eat. I didn't think it would be a good idea to eat them now."

"Thank you. I had forgotten about them until I smelled food." Cassy smiled as Colt pulled her close to him.

"I think we forgot about everything but each other for a little while. How about if we go back and pick up where we left off?"

"What and throw away this wonderful meal you just made? It would be a shame."

"It would be a shame, but it would be fun." Colt continued to kiss her neck.

"I'm sure it would be fun, but I'm starving and this looks wonderful."

Cassy wiggled out of his arms and sat down at the table smiling as Colt placed a plate of food in front of her kissing her lightly on the lips before she took a bite.

"I love you Cassy Conner."

Taken by surprise Cassy couldn't say a word. She watched the most gorgeous cowboy butt walk away from her and back to the stove. "That cowboy butt's all mine." She whispered to herself smiling.

****

"Thank you for making breakfast. It was really good." Cassy said after they both devoured the food on their plates. She picked up the dishes off the table and took them to the sink. "What's on the agenda for today?" Cassy asked as she felt Colt walk up behind her and slide his arms around her waist.

"I was thinking maybe we could spend the day in bed."

Cassy leaned back against his body. The warmth of his skin against hers brought back memories of last night. She was having a hard time concentrating on anything but him.

"What do you say?"

His moist kisses against her neck made her weak. She turned facing him and slid her arm around his neck. "Yes."

She felt him sweep her up in his arms and head down the hallway. Just as they pass the table the doorbell rang.

"Who in the hell could that be?" Colt stopped.

"I have no clue. If you put me down, I'll go check." Cassy laughed.

"I say we just pretend we didn't hear it and keep going down the hallway."

The doorbell rang again.

"They're not going away," Cassy replied. "Put me down and I'll see if I can get rid of them."

Cassy straighten her hair and robe and went to answer the door.

"Cassy Conner?"

The young delivery man asked as she opened the door.

"Yes."

"I have a certified letter for you." He handed Cassy a clipboard with an envelope attached. "Would you please sign."

Cassy signed on the line and handed him back the clipboard. She watched as he tore off the return card and handed Cassy the envelope.

"Have a nice day."

Looking at the return address on the envelope Cassy read it was from a law office.

"Who was it?" Colt asked.

"It was a delivery man with a certified letter. It's from some lawyer."

"Are you going to open it and see what it is?" Colt asked.

"Of course." Cassy slipped her finger under the edge of the envelope and opened the seal. Taking the letter out, she began reading. "You're not going to believe this."

"What?" Colt moved closer to her trying to read over her shoulder.

"I guess I have a brother," Cassy said. "According to this letter Lucas Harding is my half-brother and he wants his share of the Conner farm."

CHAPTER TWENTY

Cassy poured a cup of coffee as Colt sat at the table looking through the papers that were delivered.

"Wow, this is crazy. Did you have any idea?" Colt asked.

"No." Cassy sat down in the chair next to Colt. "I had no clue."

"Your father was a busy boy. Lucas is probably a few years older than you so that means your father was messing around with Lucas's mother around the time he married your mother."

"I really don't want to think about that part." Cassy frowned. "What it means is my father wasn't the person I thought he was."

"Your grandfather left you the Conner farm, so that tells us he had no idea he had a grandson."

"If my grandfather had no clue Lucas Harding was his grandson, then how did Lucas get the sample to do a DNA test which these papers said he did?" Cassy looked at Colt over her coffee cup.

"That's a good question. I would assume he didn't get it with your grandfather permission." Colt gave her a sideward glance.

"Correct. I guess I'm going to have to pay to have my own testing done to make sure this information is correct," Cassy said. "I'm not going to just hand over the farm my grandfather worked all of his life to build. The farm you sunk your money in to keep running. He must think I'm crazy if he thinks I'm just going to roll over and just hand him what he's asking for."

"That's the woman I fell in love with." Colt smiled.

Cassy moved from her chair and sat down in Colt's lap wrapping her arms around his neck.

"I love you, Colt Matthews." Cassy kissed him softly on the neck. "Now where did we leave off before we were so rudely interrupted by the doorbell?"

"I do believe I remember." Colt stood up from his chair taking Cassy with him in his arms. "I believe right here." Cassy held on while Colt carried her carefully down the hallway to her bedroom and laid her gently on the bed.

"Oh yes. Now I remember." Cassy laughed as Colt began undressing her.

****

"Lucas. Hi, it's Cassy Conner." Cassy shifted her cell phone from one ear to the other.

"Cassy."

"Or should I say brother?" Cassy sat down on the edge of her bed putting his business card back in the drawer of her nightstand.

"I see you received the letter from my lawyer."

"Yes. Yes, I did," Cassy replied. "So, you want half of my family farm?"

"Now that I know for sure I am family, I just want my share of what belongs to me. Nothing more," Lucas said.

"Exactly what makes you think you're my half-brother? Did my grandfather say something to you to make you think you were from this family?" Cassy wanted some answers from him. She hoped he would be honest enough to give her that much.

"No. Your grandfather never said a word and I never told him," Lucas replied.

"Who told you or gave you the idea you were a Conner?" Cassy was getting frustrated with his attitude. "I want to know the truth Lucas."

"My Mother told me."

Cassy could hear the cockiness in his voice. "Your Mother?" She remembered Lucas telling her about his mother and how she couldn't remember who he was most of the time.

"You told me your mother couldn't even remember your name most of the time. You believed her when she told you a wild story like this?"

"I didn't believe her at first." Lucas paused for a second. "She apologized to me for not having a man around when I was growing up. She thought I was missing a positive male influence." Lucas laughed. "Several times she mentioned your father and said if he hadn't run off we could've had a nice life. After her repeating herself over and over I decided I would take her serious and find out if she was telling me the truth. On one of my Emergency calls for your grandfather, I took a sample swab had it tested. You have the results."

Cassy's frustration was building. "First you have to know the sample you took was done illegally. Second, not that I don't trust you or your lawyer, but I want to have my own DNA testing done." Cassy stood and moved around the room so she would keep her voice at a normal level.

I'm going to set something up and I'll let you know where and when. I'm going to be a little more personal and give you the information you need myself instead of going through a lawyer. You know how that goes don't you?"

"You sound like you aren't too happy to find out you have a brother. After all these years of being an only child, you think you would relish the fact you have some family."

Cassy could hear Lucas laughing on the other end of the phone. "It's not that I'm unhappy to find out I have family, it's the way the family let me know. You've known for how long and we've been around each other several times since then and you choose to tell me in a letter from your lawyer. How welcoming and thoughtful of you."

"I can see we're going to be a loving family just like I thought."

"I'll let you know when and where to get testing done. I might call you with the information or I may just have it delivered by mail. It'll be a surprise," Cassy had about all of his attitude she could take.

"Not funny," Lucas replied.

"Hopefully it'll be quick and we'll get this out of the way and go on with our lives." Cassy squeezed her hand into a fist. She would love to be able to use it on Lucas.

"I'll be waiting," Lucas replied.

Cassy ended the phone call and put her cell phone down on the nightstand.

"Who was that?" Colt asked as he walked out of the shower with a towel wrapped loosely around his waist.

"It was Lucas. I called him to let him know I wanted to set up my own testing. Not that I didn't trust him, but I don't." Cassy pursed her lips and let air escape.

"What did he have to say about that?" Colt asked.

"He wasn't too happy, but who cares. All he wants is part of the farm."

"You might have to give it to him you know," Colt replied. "If he is right about being your half-brother, he could contest the will and ask for part of your grandfather's inheritance."

"He can ask all he wants. Until I'm sure he is my half-brother he gets nothing from me."

"I'd hate to mess with you lady." Colt laughed.

CHAPTER TWENTYONE

"Are you sure you don't want me to go into town with you?" Colt asked as he waited for Cassy to climb into the driver's side of the truck.

"No. I'll be all right. Thanks for volunteering though."

Colt shut the door as she reached for the seatbelt.

"Besides you've been busy with other things." Cassy winked. "There's a lot for you to catch up on around the farm."

"By other things I believe you are talking about you." Colt winked.

"Well, what can I say? You're irresistible." Cassy could feel her heart flutter. She had fallen for him with everything she had. He leaned in and gave her a kiss.

"Be careful please. Make sure you come back." Colt smiled.

"I will. I'll be expecting dinner on the table when I get home." Cassy pointed a finger in his direction.

"You got it lady." Colt stepped back and watched her drive off.

****

"I'm Cassy Conner. I have an appointment with Mr. Tomlinson."

"Yes, Ms. Conner. Mr. Tomlinson is expecting you. Have a seat and I'll let him know you are here."

Cassy sat down as the receptionist behind the desk dialed her phone. She wasn't sure exactly what she needed to do, but her grandfather trusted Alan Tomlinson so Cassy was sure he could help her. Hopefully he would keep his fees down and work quickly.

"Mr. Tomlinson will see you now, Ms. Conner. Please follow me." The receptionist walked down a long hallway to a closed door, Cassy watched as she lightly knocked and opened the door slightly. She looked in and then opened the door the rest of the way. Cassy saw an older man, who was probably around her grandfather's age, sitting behind a big wooden desk who stood as she walked in the room.

"Cassandra Conner, it's nice to meet you."

Cassy shook his hand when he walked around the desk to greet her.

"You grandfather spoke a lot about you. I feel like I know you."

"It's nice to meet you, Mr. Tomlinson." Cassy sat down in a chair in front of his desk.

"Exactly what can I do for you Cassandra?" Mr. Tomlinson asked as he walked back and took a seat in his desk chair.

"Call me Cassy, please."

"Of course, Cassy. You mentioned you need some legal advice concerning your grandfather. By the way, I was so sorry about your loss. James Conner was a wonderful person and friend."

"Thank you. I received this letter in the mail yesterday." Cassy handed him the letter across the desk. "It's was delivered to me registered mail. As you can see it's from Lucas Conner informing me his is the illegitimate son of my father. He's asking for his share of the family inheritance which means part of the Conner farm."

"I see that." Alan Tomlinson read over the letter. "Have you talked to Mr. Harding?"

"Yes. I called him to let him know I got the letter. I had some questions for him about why he thought he was a Conner and why he never mentioned anything about it until my grandfather passed."

"And his answer was?"

"He never told my grandfather because he just got the results back. His mother's the person who gave him this information. He took a sample swab from my grandfather on one of the Emergency calls he made to the farm when my grandfather was having problems."

"Well first thing we need to do is new testing. We aren't going to just take his word for it. The testing could've been compromised and the results would be bad. After we get those results back, then we'll look at what we need to do legally."

"Ok. Can you help me find where to go to do the testing?" Cassy asked.

"I'll set up the testing with the lab here at the local hospital. They will contact you and set up an appointment. It should take about three to four weeks to get the results back." Alan Tomlinson waved his hand in front of him.

"That's a long time," Cassy replied. "I guess it's all right though. I'm not in any hurry."

"It's about standard time for test results. It will give you time to adjust to the thought you may have a half-brother." Mr. Tomlinson smiled.

"I guess you're right. I'm having a hard time believing it now. It might give me some time to talk to family and some of my father and grandfather's friends who still live around here. Maybe I can get some information to help me put the pieces together from them." Cassy nodded her head.

"I'll give you a call if I need anything Cassy and we'll worry about my fees another time."

She stood up from her chair and shook Alan Tomlinson's hand.

"Thank you, Mr. Tomlinson. I'll wait for your call."

He walked her out the office door, down the hallway and out to the lobby area. He took a business card out of the holder on the receptionist's desk.

"Please call me if there is anything else I can do for you. Otherwise we'll talk when I get the results back."

"Thanks again Mr. Tomlinson."

Cassy walked out of the front door. The day hadn't built up heat yet. "I wonder."

Cassy walked down to the café only a few doors down. She sat down in the booth closest to the door. It wasn't long before Fannie greeted her with a menu.

"What brings you here at this time of the day, Hun?" Fannie asked.

"I had an appointment in town so I thought I would stop and have an early lunch before heading back to the farm." Cassy opened the menu and pretended to glance through.

"So, how's Colt these days?" Fannie placed one hand on her hip as she waited for Cassy's answer.

"He's doing well. I'll let him know you asked about him." Cassy smiled.

"You do that. Tell that handsome hunk he hasn't paid me a visit in a few weeks or so. I'm missing his lovely smile, if you know what I mean." Fannie winked at Cassy.

"Yes, I know exactly what you mean about his 'lovely smile,'" She made air quotes with her fingers. "I'll make sure he knows."

"Now what can I get you, Hun?"

"I'll have one of your delicious cheeseburgers and a diet soda." Cassy handed Fannie back the menu.

"Sure thing. It'll be out in a few minutes."

"Thanks Fannie. By the way, how many nursing homes are here in town?"

"There's only one. The Unity Nursing Home that's right off the highway as you head south." Fannie pointed in that direction.

"I know where you're talking about. So that's the only one? Thank you, Fannie."

"Are you planning on visiting someone there?" Fannie asked.

"No. I just remember someone mentioning a nursing home here before Grandpa passed away. I would volunteer at a nursing home when I lived in Texas. I thought I might do something like that here."

"Well, that's sweet of you. I'm sure those old people would love to have the company," Fannie replied. "I'll go get your order. You sit tight."

"I'll be here. Thanks for the information Fannie."

Cassy hoped Mrs. Harding was up for company because she planned to pay her a visit. Even if it meant she would return to the farm late, she needed to do this to settle some questions she had about her father only Mrs. Harding could answer.

****

"Can I help you?" The young woman behind the front desk greeted Cassy as she walked in the door of Unity Nursing home.

"Good morning," Cassy said. "I am interested in maybe doing some volunteer work. I wondered if that would be possible and who I need to talk to."

"How wonderful of you. Our residents love to have visitors. Let me find our director and you can talk to her."

"Thank you." Cassy scoped out the room and down the hallways as she waited for the receptionist to return. She noticed several residents being wheeled down the hallway. This could be interesting. She noticed the receptionist stop and talk to a woman in the hallway. She took the wheelchair from the woman then began pushing her towards the door. The woman smiled and waved at Cassy as she walked towards her.

"Hi, I'm Angela Parker. I'm the director of Unity. I understand you're interested in doing some volunteer work here."

"Yes, Ms. Parker. I'm Cassy Conner." She shook her hand. "I'm interested in volunteering. I did some volunteering when I lived in Texas. I would like to do the same here if you allow it."

"We sure do. In fact, I wish more people around town would feel like you do. The residents of Unity love to have visitors." Angela placed her hand over her heart.

"Your receptionists said the same thing. I take it you don't have many regular visitors to Unity."

"Not really. We have a few family members who visit on a regular basis, but not many other visitors. Around the holidays people feel the need to visit or we have performers come in and give shows for the residents. It depends on what our program director has lined up."

"An acquaintance of mine told me about you. I believe his mother is a residence here."

"That was nice. What's his name?" Angela asked.

"Lucas Harding. I believe his mother is a residence here."

"Of course, Lucas. He visits at least once a month, sometimes more. His mother has been here for over five years. Would you like to meet her?"

"Yes, I would love to. I told Lucas if I came to volunteer, I would make sure and visit his mother." Cassy smiled hoping her response sounded legitimate.

"Follow me." Cassy walked behind Angela as she headed down the long hallway to room three hundred."

"Hi Sarah. It's Angela. How are you doing today? You have a visitor." Angela kept talking to her as she fluffed Sarah's pillows. "Maybe you can wake up and talk to her." Angela gave Cassy a nod as if she was giving her the permission to go ahead and talk to her.

"Mrs. Harding. I'm Cassy Conner. I'm a friend of you son Lucas." Cassy sat down in the chair next to Sarah's bed and watched to see if there was any reaction to Lucas' name.

"Lucas."

Cassy could swear she heard her whisper his name. "Yes ma'am. Lucas." She watched Sarah's expression turn to a smile as she heard his name.

"She's in and out. If you talk to her you'll learn to tell if she if listening to you. Lucas picked it up right away. He's really good with her. He could probably give you some tips." Angela suggested. "I'd like to show you the rest of the nursing home. We'll see if volunteering is something you really want to do."

"Sure." Cassy stood up and walked to the door with Angela. "Goodbye Mrs. Harding. It was a pleasure to meet you."

"Lucas." Sarah whispered.

"Right down this hallway is our day room." Angela pointed down the hallway. "We like to bring our residence in here to give them a different environment for a few hours a day. We have games and activities planned by our program director."

Cassy listened to Angela tell her their schedule as they walked down the hallway. She couldn't get her mind off Sarah Harding. She wanted to talk to her longer, spend more time with her. She was a connection to her father. One she wasn't willing to let go of so soon.

CHAPTER TWENTYTWO

Colt watched through the window as the daylight began to fade. "Where the hell is she?" He opened the screen door and stepped outside. Kicking the dust around in the driveway he saw headlights in the distance.

"It's about time." He waited for Cassy to pull in the driveway and met her beside the door of the pickup. "Hey, stranger. I was worried about you."

"Hi." Cassy slid out of the pickup and hugged his neck. "I got tied up in town." She took his hand and headed for the house. "I'm starving. What's for dinner?"

"I made spaghetti and meatballs. I didn't know what time you were going to be home so all I need to do is cook the pasta." Colt smiled as Cassy walked up and slid her arms around his waist.

"You're the most wonderful man. I don't know how I got so lucky." Her eyes glowed when she looked at him.

"I'm the lucky one." Colt pulled her close, lightly touching her lips with his. He could feel her body responding to his touch. He kissed her harder as he heard her sigh.

"Are you still hungry?"

"Yes." She laid her head on his shoulder and let out a long sigh.

"Let me make you something to eat." Colt laughed as he put his arm around her waist and began walking toward the house.

"I thought you would never offer," Cassy replied.

"You said you got tied up in town. What tied you up?" Colt opened the screen door for her.

"I talked to the lawyer. He's going to set up testing time for Lucas and I and let me know. He said I could worry about his fees another time." Cassy paused for a minute. "I also stopped by the Unity Nursing Home."

"Why did you stop there?" Colt turned the fire up under the water for the pasta.

"I met Sarah Harding, Lucas's mother." Cassy smiled at him. "I've been thinking about her ever since I got the letter from Lucas saying he was my half-brother. Since I was in town, I thought I would try to meet her."

"She has dementia, right? Why would you want to meet her?" Colt was confused on what Cassy thought she was going to get out of her. He remembered Lucas telling him his mother was out of it most of the time.

"Lucas mentioned there were some moments when she was lucid. She would remember who he was and everything." Cassy leaned against the kitchen counter. "I thought maybe if I met her and gained her trust, she would maybe share some memories with me about my father."

"You really think she has something to tell you about you father you don't already know?" Colt dropped pasta in the boiling water.

"I'm not sure, but it's worth a try." Cassy shrugged her shoulders "If what Lucas said is true and he's my half-brother, she knew my father when he was younger."

Colt watched as she turned her gaze to the floor and looked as if she was lost in thought.

"I just thought I would see how she was different from my mother." Cassy finally spoke.

"You really want to know that?" Colt laughed. "He married your mother, not Sarah Harding. Your father might have not even known she was pregnant with Lucas or maybe she's lying about his father."

"You right. He did marry my mother and not Sarah, but there had to be something about her he liked maybe even loved?"

"I hope you don't go digging up my old girlfriends to find out about them." Colt leaned over and nudged her with his elbow.

"Very funny. Speaking of old girlfriends, Fannie told me you need to get your gorgeous smile into the café and see her. It's been way too long." Cassy patted him on the hand.

"Fannie. She's one of kind. If I hadn't fallen for you, she was my next choice." Colt stirred the pasta.

"That's really good to know."

Colt take her hand and pull her to him. She curled up against him, kissing him on the neck running her hand down his chest. How she knew exactly what he liked, he didn't know but she could always make him give in.

"Can Fannie do this?" Cassy whispered.

"I don't think so." Colt sighed as she kissed his neck right where she knew he liked. "I love you, Cassy."

"I love you too, Colt."

Colt let out a soft moan as she kissed him gently on the lips.

"I'm starving and dinner smells wonderful."

"Good." Colt held her tight. "Fannie taught me how to make it."

CHAPTER TWENTYTHREE

Cassy pulled into a parking spot in front of the doctor's office. She was a few minutes early for her appointment, but she knew there would be paperwork involved. As she walked up to the front door, Lucas came walking out.

"Well, well. Look's who's here." Lucas grinned. "It's been awhile, Sis."

"Lucas." Cassy waited for him to walk out the door before she started through.

"See you around." Cassy kept going without saying a word.

"You can be so arrogant." She whispered as she watched him climb in his truck and drive away.

"Cassy Conner. I have a ten o'clock appointment."

"Sure Ms. Conner. Would you please fill out these papers on the back and front? Also, I'll need a copy of your insurance card."

Cassy took her wallet out of her purse and handed the nurse her insurance card. She watched as the nurse took a quick scan and handed it back to her. She found an empty seat in the waiting area and began filling out the forms.

"Ms. Conner. The doctor will see you now." A nurse called her from a side door of the waiting area. "Follow me."

Cassy followed her back to a room where she climbed up on an exam table and waited. A tall, attractive, well dressed female doctor entered the room.

"Cassy Conner? I'm Dr. Jones. I understand you're here for some testing."

Cassy watched as the tall, slender woman wearing a white coat over her blouse and slacks her blonde hair pulled back in a ponytail, sit on a rolling stool and move close to the exam table. The nurse with her was putting on rubber gloves and handing the doctor a pair. She opened up a sealed paper packet and pulled out what looked to Cassy like a long Q-tip and handed it to the doctor.

"Open wide. This will only take a few seconds and we'll be done."

Cassy open her mouth as Dr. Jones rubbed the swab inside her mouth and under her tongue. The nurse opened a long plastic container which she had placed a sticker on the outside. Dr. Jones dropped the swab in the plastic bag then the nurse seal it closed.

"Well, that's all there is to it." Dr. Jones smiled. "We should have the results back in three to four weeks." The nurse picked up everything from the cabinet and headed out the door.

"Thank you, Dr. Jones. Will you call me with the results or will they go directly to my lawyer?" Cassy asked.

"The results will come directly from the lab and go to your lawyer."

"Great." Cassy kicked her feet as she waited for Dr. Jones to leave.

"Lucas is a good guy. You could do worse than to have him for a half-brother," Dr. Jones replied.

"Really? How do you know Lucas?" Cassy waited for her reply.

"Let's just say, he's a close friend of mine. We met at the hospital."

"That's make sense. He's a paramedic and you're a doctor. Perfect match?" Cassy laughed.

"Something like that," Dr. Jones smiled. "His mother is also a patient of mine."

"Lucas told me about his mother. I met her yesterday when I toured the nursing home."

"You toured Unity Nursing Home? I thought your grandfather passed."

"He did. I was thinking about volunteering there in my free time." Cassy explained.

"That would be nice. They could use some volunteers. Not many people in this town think it's important to even visit their own relatives, much less strangers. I know the residents appreciate the company. I know they love it when I come to visit. They're all full of stories."

"Lucas told me his mother has moments where she remembers him. That has to be so hard from him to visit and not have her remember who he is." Cassy tried to imagine.

"I'm sure it is. It would be hard for me." Dr. Jones stood and placed her hands in her pockets. "It was nice to meet you Cassy. I hope everything turns out like you want it. You seem to be a nice person."

"Thanks, Dr. Jones. Good luck with Lucas. I'll put in a good word for you." Cassy climbed off the exam table, picked up her purse and headed for her car.

****

"Hi, Ms. Conner. It's good to see you again." Angela Parker came out of her office to greet Cassy. "I didn't expect you back so soon."

"I was in town for an appointment so I thought I would stop by. I don't have much time, but I thought I could pay a visit to a few of the residents. Maybe take them for a walk, if that's all right with you. It's a beautiful day."

"That's perfectly fine with me."

"I'd like to stop in and see Sarah Harding first." Cassy waved her hand in the direction of her room.

"She would love that. You remember her room?" Angela asked.

"Yes. Thank you, Angela. Maybe I'll see you before I leave." Cassy headed down the hallway towards room three hundred. She walked through the doorway and noticed Sarah Harding sitting up in the chair next to her bed. Cassy sat down in the empty chair next to her.

"Hi again, Ms. Harding. Do you remember me?" Cassy didn't notice any movement from her. "I'm a friend of your son, Lucas." Cassy reminded her.

"Lucas." Sarah Harding whispered.

"Yes, Lucas." Cassy repeated. "I just ran into Lucas this morning."

"You saw my son? Is he here?" Sarah smiled a small amount.

"He's not here, Ms. Harding." Cassy placed her hand on Sarah's knee. "He'll probably stop by soon. I saw him at the doctor this morning."

"Is Lucas all right? Why was he at the doctor?"

"He's fine. Lucas is fine. He was there for a checkup that's all."

"Good. He's all right. Good." Sarah nodded her head. "I worry about him."

"How are you, Ms. Harding? Are you feeling all right?" Cassy watched the expression on her face relax.

"Yes dear. I'm fine. You look lovely today. How do you know my Lucas?"

"I met Lucas when he helped my grandfather."

"Was your grandfather sick?" Sarah asked.

"Yes, he was, but Lucas helped him and he was fine after that." Cassy smiled.

"Do you remember my grandfather, Ms. Harding? His name was James Conner." Cassy watched her expression for any change.

"James Conner." Sarah Harding seemed surprised. "You belong to James Conner?"

"I'm his granddaughter. He passed away several weeks ago." Cassy explained.

"Lucas told me. I'm sorry. He told me he killed him."

Cassy couldn't believe what she was hearing. Surely Sarah Harding didn't know what she was talking about. There was no change to her expression. Cassy took her cell phone out of her purse and pushed the memo record button.

"What do you mean, Ms. Harding? Why would Lucas kill my grandfather?" Cassy asked.

"Shhh." Sarah Harding placed one of her fingers up against her lips. "It's a secret. Lucas told me not to say anything to anyone."

"It's all right Ms. Harding, Lucas and I are friends. You can tell me anything." Cassy whispered.

"Lucas snuck in James Conner's house and gave him a shot. Lucas said James didn't fight him. He told James he was taking care of him. It was easy Lucas said. James trusted him."

The blank expression on Sarah Harding's face gave Cassy a chill. "Why would Lucas do something like that Ms. Harding?"

"He wants to give me a nice home. Lucas deserves that farm. After all he was supposed to be a Conner you know. If his father would have married me instead of that other bitch, Lucas would have what he deserves. Instead, he has to get rid of that girl that lives there now and some farmhand so he can have it all. He promised me he would make a room for me when he finally got rid of everyone who doesn't belong." The smile on Sarah Harding face grew larger.

"Are you sure about that Mrs. Harding? Do you remember the girl's name?"

"How could I forget? Her name was the same as yours. It was Cassy." Sarah Harding pointed her finger at her.

Cassy couldn't say anything. Her heart was in her throat and beating fast. She stopped the recording on her phone, picked up her purse and backed slowly out of the room without saying anything. The expression on Sarah Harding's face didn't change at all. She was talking about her son killing a man and her expression didn't change. Was she telling the truth? Cassy wanted to run. No, she needed to run. She wanted to get to Colt as fast as she could. She needed him now.

"Are you all right, Cassy?" She could hear Angela Parker's voice coming from down the hallway. Cassy took a few deep breaths to try and keep calm. She needed to calm down. She didn't want to tell anyone else about what Sarah Harding said, not until she talked to Colt.

"I'm fine, Angela. I just remembered, I have somewhere else I need to be. I'll have to come back again when I have some more time." Cassy could feel her heart beat slowing down to a normal pace. Her breathing was becoming normal. She hoped the color had returned to her face.

"That would be great, Cassy. It's so nice of you to spend some of your free time with us."

"Next time I'll try to let you know before I show up," Cassy replied. "I've really got to go." Cassy headed down the hallway to the front door. Angela walked with her.

"Cassy. Imagine running into you here?" Lucas was standing right in front of her. "First the doctor's office and now here at Unity."

"Lucas."

"What are you doing here, Cassy? You don't know anyone in this nursing home."

"I don't." Cassy took a breath before she said anything else. "I was in town and I remembered you talking about your mother being in a nursing home. I always volunteered when I lived in Texas. I thought maybe I could do the same here at Unity." Cassy hoped he was buying everything she was saying. She felt like she was a little kid with her hand caught in the cookie jar.

"Cassy's really doing us a favor and the residence love it." Angela smiled.

"How nice of you," Lucas replied.

"By the way, Angela introduced me to your mother. She's a very nice lady."

"You talked to my mom?" Lucas asked.

"Not really." Cassy scrunched up her nose. "She didn't have much to say. She did seem to come alive when I mentioned your name."

"Nothing like a mother's love," Lucas replied.

"I've really got to go. I have to meet Colt back at the farm." Cassy started walking toward the front door as calmly as she could. The last thing she needed was Lucas suspecting anything. "See you around, Lucas. It was nice to see you again, Angela."

"You too, Cassy," Angela said. "I'll see you soon."

Opening the truck door Cassy slipped in the seat, took her keys out of her purse and started the truck. She couldn't wait to get home to Colt. She had to tell someone about her visit with Sarah Harding before she exploded. That someone was Colt. It's a good think she got it recorded on her cell phone or no one would believe her.

CHAPTER TWENTYFOUR

"Colt." Cassy slid out of the truck and slammed the door. "Colt. Where are you?" She didn't see him anywhere outside the house or barn so she headed for the house. Opening the back door, she ran in looking around the kitchen and living room.

"Colt. Are you in here?" There was no answer so Cassy headed back outside. He had to be here somewhere. She saw him walking towards her from the barn.

"There you are." Cassy ran towards him.

"What's going on? Colt asked as she reached him out of breath. "Are you all right?"

"Yes. Come with me. I have something I need to show you." Cassy grabbed Colt's arm and started heading towards the house.

"What's going on Cassy? How did your appointment in town go? Is that what this is all about?" Colt tried to keep up.

"I'll tell you everything, but let's go in the house." Cassy kept hurrying toward the door.

"Okay. I guess."

Cassy kept pulling Colt towards the house almost at a trout. They walked in the backdoor and Cassy pointed to the chair at the kitchen table for Colt to sit down.

"I don't know what happened to you in town today, but I can't wait to hear this." Colt laughed.

Cassy sat down in the chair next to him. "I went to my doctor's appointment this morning and I ran into Lucas as I was going in the building. He must've just finished his appointment. Dr. Jones and I talked as she was taking care of my DNA test and I learned she was Sarah Harding's doctor."

"Sarah Harding, Lucas' mother?" Colt asked.

"Yes. Anyway, I decided I would stop by the Unity Nursing Home on my way out of town and visit with Sarah Harding again."

"Cassy." Colt took off his hat and placed it on the table then ran his fingers through his hair. "So how was she today?"

"Listen for yourself?" Cassy pulled her cell phone out of her purse and played the memo recording for Colt. When it was finished, she looked at the expression on Colt's face. "What do you think?"

"She told you Lucas was responsible for your grandfather's death so he could inherit the Conner farm for her? Now he's planning to do something to get me and you out of the way so he can have the entire farm?" Colt asked.

Cassy could tell by the expression on Colt's face he was just as shocked by Sarah Harding's story as she was.

"Do you think we should believe her?" Cassy asked. "I mean Lucas said she had times of lucid thinking and would remember him and her surroundings. Do you think she's telling me the truth?"

"I don't know what to say, Cassy. It sounds like the rambling of an old woman who's crazy. I don't know if anyone is going to believe it."

"Do we just forget about it and go on like nothing happened?" Cassy sat back in her chair.

"Boy, Cassy, I'm not sure what to do." Colt ran his hands through his hair again. "I would be afraid to just forget about it. What if the old woman was telling the truth?"

"I'm going to call Detective Sloan and Rogers and see what they think." Cassy stood up from the table. "I don't know about you, but Sarah Harding scared me, Colt. I can't just forget about it."

As Colt took her in his arms, she could feel his heart beating almost as fast as hers. She knew he didn't like what he heard any more than she did.

****

"Detective Sloan, Detective Rogers." Cassy smiled as the two men walked up to the front door. "Please, come in and have a seat." Cassy moved aside as they both walked in the living room and sat down on the couch.

"Ms. Conner. Your call sounded important. What is it we can do for you this time?" Detective Sloan and Rogers both pulled out small notebooks and a pen from their jacket pockets.

Cassy heard Colt walk in the back down of the house. She waited for him to sit down in the chair next to her before she continued. "You remember Colt Matthews?"

"Yes, we do. Is it all right from him to hear what we have to discuss?" Detective Sloan asked.

"Yes. I want Colt here because this involves him also," Cassy replied.

"If it's fine with you, then go ahead." Detective Sloan nodded.

"I was in town yesterday so I stopped at the Unity Nursing Home. I paid a visit to Sarah Harding."

"Sarah Harding?" Detective Sloan asked. "Isn't she Lucas Harding's mother?"

"Yes." Cassy nodded.

"Why would you go visit her?" Detective Rogers asked.

"Lucas mentioned his mother was in Unity Nursing Home and I was interested in doing some volunteer work. When I lived in Texas, I tried to volunteer as much time as I could at the local nursing homes. Anyway, I wanted to continue doing the same since I moved back here, especially after losing my grandfather. This was the second visit I had with Sarah Harding."

"You'd been to visit her before?" Detective Rogers asked as he made notes in his notebook.

"Yes, once for just a short visit. This visit was different." Cassy took her cell phone out of her pocket and played the memo recording for the two detectives. When it was finished she left it lay on the table.

"What do you think?" Cassy looked at each of the Detectives.

"That was Sarah Harding? What made you decided to record what she was saying?" Detective Sloan asked.

"I'm not sure" Cassy thought back to when she was sitting across from Sarah Harding. "It was the look on her face and when I mentioned I was a friend of Lucas, she seemed to come alive. I thought maybe she would say something I could play back to Lucas to make him feel good."

"Well, I'd say what you recorded certainly isn't something Lucas is going to be proud of." Detective Rogers laughed.

"Mr. Matthews, didn't you tell us you were playing pool with Lucas Harding the night James Conner passed?" Detective Rogers asked Colt.

"Yes. I was at the bar that night. I had a few beers and played a few games of pool after dinner," Colt replied.

"You said you started not feeling well so you headed back to the farm, right?" Detective Sloan looked flipped through the pages in his notebook.

"Yes. That's right. I pulled over because I got sick and then passed out in the truck. When I woke up I drove the rest of the way to the farm, unloaded the supplies and went to bed."

"You never told me that, Colt." Cassy looked at him. "Why didn't you tell me about being sick?"

"It was nothing. I just thought I drank too much and I shouldn't have been driving. When I think back I only had a couple of beers. There's no way what I drank could have made me pass out," Colt replied.

"Maybe we should talk to a few people who were at the bar with you and Lucas that night," Detective Rogers replied.

"Do you mind if we take your phone and copy the recording you made? We'll return it to you as soon as we can." Detective Sloan asked as he pointed to the phone lying on the table.

"Sure. Take it if it'll help." Cassy picked up her cell phone and handed it to Detective Sloan.

"We would like to do some investigating. Maybe talk to Mrs. Harding on our own." Both Detectives stood up from the couch and headed towards the front door.

"What do we do now?" Cassy stood up and put her arms around Colt as they walked the detectives to the front door.

"I would suggest you guys do nothing. I wouldn't talk to anyone about this, but I would suggest you take a few precautions like locking your doors during the day and at night, know where each of you are at all times." Detective Sloan suggested.

"We'll wait to hear from you then." Cassy looked at Colt both detectives climb into their car and drove off. She hugged Colt as tight as she could. She was afraid for him as much as she was for herself.

CHAPTER TWENTYFIVE

Dinner was quiet. Colt tried to make conversation to break the silence. Since Detective's Sloan and Rogers left, he hadn't let Cassy out of his site. He insisted she go with him to finish the chores on the farm. When they finished, they showered then started dinner. Cassy wasn't hungry, but she didn't want to hurt Colt's feelings. He'd gone to the trouble of frying chicken, making mashed potatoes and gravy.

"Thank you for making dinner. It's really good. Your fried chicken's much better than mine. You're going to have to teach me how to make it."

"It's a family secret passed down from my grandmother's grandmother. I don't think I can give it to you." Cassy saw that cute smile on his face, the corner of his mouth turned up. She loved his smile. It was the first thing she noticed about him and it made her body react putting her at ease.

"Really. Exactly what do I have to do to get the recipe?" Cassy leaned over and took his hand.

"The first thing you have to do is marry me." Colt replied. "Unless your last name is Matthews you'll never get it."

Cassy dropped her fork on the table. "Did you just ask me to marry you Colt Matthews?"

"Yes, I believe I did. What do you say?" Colt picked her up out of her chair. "You know I'm crazy about you."

"Yes, I'll marry you Colt. I love you, too." She laughed as he twirled her around the kitchen floor.

"Well, well. Isn't this a sweet moment? I'm glad I was here to share it."

Cassy and Colt stopped and turned to catch Lucas Harding standing right inside the back door.

"Lucas." Cassy exclaimed. "What are you doing here?"

"I thought I would stop by and see how my half-sister and future business partner was doing. It looks like you guys are doing great. Are we celebrating something?"

The look on his face told Cassy he was here for something more than checking up on them. "Colt just asked me to marry him."

"Well congratulations you two." Lucas walked in the kitchen and grabbed a piece of chicken from the platter on the table and took a bite. "This is good stuff. You're marrying a great cook, Colt."

"Actually, Colt fried the chicken. I'm the one marrying the great cook." Cassy quickly corrected him.

"I'm just learning all kinds of things about you two. It'll come in handy when I move in the take over my share of the farm."

"What do you want Lucas?" Cassy was becoming frustrated with his attitude. She also noticed the expression on Colt's face changed. He wasn't happy with the conversation. "And while we're at it, how did you get in the house? I locked the back door."

"I know where you keep the spare key. I had to use it a few times when old man Conner was alive. He told me where it was just in case we couldn't get in the house on one of our calls. I have to give the old man his props. He was always prepared."

"Lucas, my lawyer said the results of our testing wouldn't be back for another three to four weeks. After that, we still have to go through processes. It'll probably by six months to a year before everything is settled legally. Aren't you jumping the gun a little bit coming out here?" Cassy took the plates off the table and carried them to the sink.

"What, you guys aren't going to finish your dinner? Don't tell me it because of me." A creepy sound came from Lucas which didn't seem like a laugh. Cassy could feel the chill run up her spine. It was almost the same feeling she had when she visited Sarah Harding yesterday. She knew she had to keep her cool and get him to leave before Colt became really angry.

"We just finished eating right before you walked in the door. I'm just going to clean up." Cassy picked up some more empty plates off the table and carried them to the sink. She noticed Lucas stand up from the table and walk into the living room. He stopped and looked around.

"It looks like I'll get the old man's room when I move in. You two are shacking up together right?" He waved his piece of chicken in the air taking turns pointed at each of them.

"Exactly what the hell do you want, Harding?" Colt asked.

Cassy walked up beside Colt and placed her hand on his chest to calm him. "If and when that time comes, we'll discuss that. Until then, my grandfather's stuff stays right where it is." Cassy was now getting frustrated with Lucas' attitude. "Is there some reason you're here other than to be annoying?" Cassy asked.

"Annoying? I don't think I'm being annoying. I'm just looking to the future and how things are going to work." Lucas kept walking around the room.

"You go ahead and plan all you want, but I don't believe it's going to work out like you think it's going to." Cassy dried her hands on the kitchen towel she had taken off the oven door. "You seem to think you're going to move in here and just take over. It's not going to work that way." Cassy explained. "I don't think you're ever going to own any of the Conner farm.

"You have spitfire here, Colt. I bet that's what you love about her." Lucas smiled and winked at Colt.

Cassy's body stiffened as she could feel her cheeks heating up. Lucas had succeeded in pissing her off and she wasn't going to put up with much more. Just as she was ready to tell him exactly what she thought of his comments, Colt took her by the shoulders and grounded her in her place.

"Lucas, I think you need to leave. You've overstayed your welcome." Colt's voice contained his anger. "Drop the spare key on the table before you leave."

"I can't believe I'm not welcome in my own future home." Lucas dropped the key in his hand on the table.

Cassy felt Colt push her to the side and step between Lucas and her. "Let's go." He took Lucas by the arm and led him towards the door.

"It was good to see you again, Sis. Don't worry, it won't be that long before you and I'll see each other again. Maybe next time it'll be just you and me and you won't have a body guard."

There was that evil laugh again. Cassy watched Colt push Lucas out the door towards his truck. Lucas lost his balance and almost fell. Colt didn't move. He stood frozen in place.

"Colt." Cassy yelled. "He's not worth getting upset over. Come back in the house."

"Not until he leaves."

Cassy knew Colt wasn't going to budge until Lucas was in his truck, past the end of the driveway and out of sight. Cassy walked outside and put her arms around his waist.

"What are we going to do, Colt? Lucas is going to keep it up until he owns part of the farm or lives here with us. I don't think I can handle that."

"The first thing we're going to do is change the damn locks on all the doors."

CHAPTER TWENTYSIX

Cassy gave up trying to sleep. She glanced at the clock and it read six am. She slipped quietly out of bed so to not wake Colt. He insisted on staying with her last night. After he'd gone around the house and closed all the downstairs windows and double bolted the back and front doors. There was no way anyone could've gotten into the house during the night without waking either one of them. Wrapping in her bathrobe, she headed down the hall to make coffee and start breakfast. She walked around the house opening windows on the lower level to let the breeze blow through. It was going to heat up by early afternoon. The sooner she could cool down the house the better.

The coffee was done and she was cooking some bacon on the stove. She opened a can of biscuits and placed them in the oven.

"It smells wonderful in here."

Cassy turned to see Colt walking down the hallway, shirtless, buttoning his jeans. He was gorgeous and every time she looked at him she realized how lucky she was and he loved her.

"I wasn't sleeping very well so I thought I would give up on it and come make breakfast. How about some eggs, bacon and biscuits?" Cassy went back to attending her bacon.

"That'll be great. What can I do?"

Cassy felt him walk up behind her and put his arms around her waist, kissing her neck. "You can keep doing that all you want."

"That's fine with me, but that won't get your breakfast eaten."

"Ok, then why don't you hand me two plates then put some silverware and napkins on the table please." Cassy was disappointed when he moved away.

"Wow, I thought maybe after last night I'd earned breakfast in bed." He reached for two plates from the cabinet.

Cassy turned around to face him. "You were wonderful last night. Not quite breakfast in bed material though." She pointed her spatula at him.

"Ouch, that hurt. I thought I was at the top of my game." Colt sighed a dramatic sigh.

"I think you were still a little distracted by our visitor last night."

"You mean Lucas. Maybe you're right. I kept waking up all night making sure everything was quiet. I think I even got up a few times and walked around the house. Everything about last night pissed me off." Colt sat the plates on the cabinet next to Cassy.

"We really shouldn't be letting him or what his mother said get to us. I don't think he's stupid enough to try and take both of us out so he can inherit the ranch." Cassy took the eggs from the refrigerator and whipped them up in a bowl before emptying them into the pan.

"Your right, I know. He's surely not crazy enough to try something."

Cassy took two glasses out of the cabinet and handed them to Colt. While Colt poured each of them a glass of milk, she took the biscuits out of the oven and scrambled the eggs. She put the plates of eggs with a biscuit and a few slices of bacon on the table and sat down in one of the empty chairs.

"What do you have to do today around the farm?" Cassy asked as Colt sat down next to her handing her a glass of milk.

"I have lots of chores. I've been a little distracted this past week." Cassy felt Colt's hand pat her leg. "Why don't you come help me? We can finish before lunch then we can drive into town and have lunch at the café. We can have a delicious cheeseburger and I can see Fannie. I'll kill two birds with one stone." Colt took a drink of his milk.

"Really?" Cassy smiled. "You think so."

"I know Fannie would've been happy with my performance even if it wasn't on top of my game."

Cassy laughed so hard she spurted milk through her nose. "Now I'm in competition with Fannie. That's nice to know."

Colt took her hand in his. "I thought we could stop at the jeweler in town and see if we can find a diamond to go on that finger."

"Are you serious?" Cassy's eyebrows raised.

"Very serious. How about it?" Colt winked.

"You have a deal." Cassy jumped up from her chair and hugged Colt's neck. "You make me very happy Colt Matthews."

"So then go get your work clothes on the let's get started on the chores. How well you're on top of your game today will determine the size of rock that'll go on that finger."

"So that's how it's going to be huh?" Cassy popped him on the shoulder.

"I thought I would give it a try. It seemed to work for you this morning."

"You're out of you league, Colt Matthews. Don't even try to compete with the pro." Cassy jumped up from Colt's lap and started down the hallway. "I'll meet you in here after I've changed. Make sure you take care of the breakfast dishes."

"Not funny, Cassy. That diamond's getting smaller and smaller."

****

Cassy was hot and sweaty from the heat of the day, but also from spending the morning watching a shirtless Colt take care of chores around the farm. She helped as much as she could. Most of her time was spent admiring Colt and his spectacular build. He would catch her looking and laugh. Cassy knew he realized what she was doing and was putting on a show for her and she loved it.

"Are we done yet?" Cassy asked as Colt climbed back on the four-wheeler. "We've checked the fence, made sure the cattle were still grazing in the pasture you want them in, chased a few of them out of the pond. What's left?"

"If you're going to be a cattle farmer, you're going to have to tough it up lady." Colt laughed.

"That's what I have you for. I'm never going to be able to keep up with you. I'm not even going to try." Cassy brushed some sweat off her forehead.

"I see. I'm not only eye candy, but your chore boy." Colt smiled.

"You love it and you know it." Cassy put her arms around Colt's waist. "Take me home, have your way with me and then take me into town and buy me that diamond."

"You got it lady."

Cassy felt Colt reeve up the four-wheeler and take off. Before she knew it, they were back at the house.

CHAPTER TWENTYSEVEN

They both showered and dressed and as usual, Colt sat at the kitchen table waiting for Cassy to finish dressing. When she came down the hallway, he whistled from the kitchen.

"Thanks." Cassy kissed him on the cheek. "Are you ready to go?"

"I've been ready for half an hour. I've been waiting on you." Colt laughed. "And, I must say, you're totally worth the wait."

"That's so sweet of you." Cassy snuggled up next to him. She smelled wonderful and felt almost as good.

"Are you ready to go? I'm starving and we want to have time at the jeweler before they close." Colt patted her on the buttocks.

"I'm ready."

He felt Cassy grab his arms before he got too far away from her.

"Are you sure about this Colt?"

He could see she was serious by the look in her eyes. Taking her in his arms, he kissed her. "I'm positive. I love you Cassy Conner."

"Let's go then." Cassy ran out the back door and he wasn't far behind.

Colt watched as Cassy jumped in the passenger side of his truck. He slid behind the wheel right behind her.

"Buckle you seat belt." Colt pointed to the belt hanging beside her.

"You know I hate seat belts," Cassy replied. "They wrinkle my clothes."

"I don't care if you don't like them." Colt reached across the seat and buckled her seat belt. "You're wearing it."

"You really do love me."

He leaned in closer and kissed her. "Yes, I do."

"I trust your driving." Cassy unhooked her seatbelt smiling at Colt.

Colt shook his head as he started the engine and headed out the driveway to the road. Rolling up the windows, he set the air conditioner to a comfortable temp and turned the radio up. Cassy liked to sing along with the radio and she had a beautiful voice.

She could sing as well as some of the popular country singers he listened to. He tried to get her to come along with him and sing at the karaoke contests at the bar in town, positive she would beat out all the other singers. One of her favorite songs came on the radio and she started singing along.

Colt smiled and listened trying to keep his eyes on the road and pay attention to Cassy. He noticed another truck coming atop the hill. Colt pulled over closer to the side of the road and tapped the brakes.

"Shit!" Colt exclaimed.

"What's wrong?" Cassy asked.

"I don't know." Colt tightened his grip on the steering wheel. He could feel his body tense up as he pumped the brakes. There was nothing. They pushed all the way through to the floor board. He had to keep his cool. He couldn't get Cassy upset. All he could do was try to control the truck until it slowed down. The gravel on the country road wasn't giving him much help. There was no side road to drive off. There was nothing but trees, fences and ditches along the way. Colt tried his best to stay out of the ditches.

"Colt, slow down!" Cassy shouted.

"I'm trying Cassy. I don't have any brakes."

"What do you mean no brakes? You mean we can't stop?"

"I'm trying to slow down and it's not working. I need to find something to run into that won't kill us. Put your seatbelt on." Just as Colt's words left his mouth a dump truck came at them from over the next incline. Colt moved closer to the edge of the road to give him room to pass. As soon as he hit the edge, he could feel the gravel pulling them into the ditch.

"Hold on Cassy. I'm losing control."

The next thing Colt remembered was the truck rolling into the ditch and flipping over. They came to rest in a farm field. Colt was stunned. He tried to lift his head to find Cassy. He didn't hear anything coming from her side of the truck. He began to call out hoping she would hear him. "Cassy. Cassy, where are you?

Colt still didn't hear anything coming from her side of the truck. Colt tried to move his arms and unhooked his seat belt.

"Hey man. Are you all right?" Colt heard a voice coming from outside the truck.

"Don't move. We've called an ambulance and they'll be here soon."

Colt could see a young man looking in the windshield of the truck.

"How's my fiancé?" Colt asked as he finally managed to move enough to be able to turn and check for Cassy.

"Where is she?" Colt didn't see Cassy anywhere. The passenger door of the truck was gone and so was Cassy.

"Where the hell is she?" Colt screamed looking up at the young man. He tried to move his legs but they were stuck.

"Go find my fiancé." Colt yelled at the young man. "She was in the truck with me. Oh my god. Please, go find her."

"I'll go look. Stay calm man. The ambulance will be here in a minute. I'll go look." Colt watched as the kid disappeared into the field. It seemed forever before he came back.

"Did you find her?" Colt asked. He could tell by the look on the kids face it wasn't going to be good news.

"Yeah man. I found her. She's must have been thrown from the truck. She's still alive, but she's unconscious."

Colt heard the words, but didn't want them to register. He tried to move his legs again, but no luck. He beat his hands against the steering wheel in frustration.

"Go stay with her until they get here, please. I'm fine. Just make sure she's all right." Colt could feel the tears running down his cheeks. "Go, make sure she's all right."

"I will. You stay calm. I'll go stay with her and make sure the rescue people know where she is. Stay calm man. They're almost here."

Colt watched the kid disappear in the field again. He finally could hear the sirens in the distance. He just had to keep his cool until they could get to Cassy. All he could do right now was pray.

****

Colt woke to the sound of metal crunching. He looked up to see a fireman working to pry him out of the truck. He's legs were stuck underneath the steering column. He could feel the sharp pains shooting through his legs with each crunch of the metal. There was a paramedic inside the cab of the truck with Colt. He had crawled through the passenger side of the truck which had lost the door and Cassy.

"How's Cassy." Colt managed to get the words out.

"Is Cassy the woman with you?" The paramedic asked.

"Yes. How is she?" Colt tensed up as the pain grew.

"They're checking her out now."

"Is she all right?" Colt asked waiting for answer from either one of the men.

"I wish I could say for sure. They're working on her and I'm here with you. Let's get you out and then I'll go find out for you." The paramedic finally answered.

"Then hurry up and get me the hell out of here. I need to know if she's all right." Colt tried to move, but was stopped by a shooting pain up his leg.

"We're working as hard as we can. You're going to have to stay still so we can do that. It'll be just a few more minutes. Let's concentrate on you right now, Okay?" The paramedic insisted.

Colt took a deep breath. He could feel the frustration building and he had to keep it in control. He needed to get to Cassy and that's all he could think about right now.

"He's free. Let's get him out." The paramedic in the cab with Colt yelled. The fireman outside the cab opened the driver's door and grabbed Colt under the arms pulling him backwards out of the cab. Colt flinched with every inch they moved him. The pain was shooting through each of his legs.

"As soon as we get you out, I can check you better and I can give you something for the pain. Just hang in there a few more minutes man. Okay?"

Colt could only nod to the paramedic in the cab with him acknowledging his request. He felt them put him on a stretcher and begin moving him out of the field. He looked around trying to find Cassy, but he couldn't see her anywhere.

"Where's Cassy." Colt asked as they began to put him in the ambulance. "Where's Cassy?" He grabbed the arm of the paramedic next to him.

"They've already taken her to the hospital. She'll be there when we get you there."

"How is she? Is she all right?" Colt tried to ask as they were putting an oxygen mask on him.

"She had some nasty injuries. She was thrown from the truck. They'll know more when they get her to the hospital. Now let's get you there so we can check you out better," The paramedic replied.

Colt lay back on the stretcher as a paramedic climbed in the ambulance with him. He watched the two firemen shut the doors and they drove away. All he wanted right now was Cassy. He needed to know if she was all right and he couldn't get anyone to answer him. He didn't care what was wrong with him. He needed to know about Cassy.

****

Colt wanted to climb off the table and go search the hospital for Cassy. He knew she was here, but he didn't know where or how she was. No one would tell him anything. If he could make his legs cooperate, he would. He could hear the nurses and doctors talking, asking for tests to be done and for blood to be drawn. He just wanted to find Cassy.

"Mr. Matthews. I'm Dr. Williams. You're a very lucky man. You seem to be checking out all right. Just a few bumps and brushes and a broken leg."

"A broken leg?" Colt asked. "That's great. How am I going to take care of the farm with a broken leg?"

"We'll worry about that later. Right now, you need to rest. We want to run some more tests and take some more x-rays."

"I need to go home and take care of the farm. When do I get out of here?" Colt asked.

"We need to keep you at least overnight. You might have to make arrangements for the farm until we can let you go," Dr. Williams said.

"I'm not as much worried about the farm. I want to know about Cassy Conner. Where is she? How is she?"

"Cassy had a few more injuries than you. She's in the next room being checked out by Dr. Jones. I promise as soon as Dr. Jones knows anything she'll be in here to talk to you."

"Is Cassy all right? That's all I need to know. Is she all right?" Colt asked.

"She's stable for now. From what I can tell and what Dr. Jones has said, she hit her head pretty hard but she's a very lucky young lady. She doesn't have any broken bones, just several of bumps and bruises. She wasn't wearing her seat belt, was she?" Dr. Williams asked.

"No. I tried to get her to put it on, but she wouldn't. She said it wrinkled her clothes. I don't know why I didn't make her put it on." Colt closed his eyes as he thought back to how he let her leave it unhooked.

"Next time you will." Dr. Williams patted him on the arm.

"You bet your ass I will," Colt replied.

****

"You have a visitor, Cassy." The nurse smiled as she wheeled Colt through the hospital room door.

"Colt." Cassy whispered.

"Cassy. I'm right here." Cassy felt him reach out and take her hand in his kissing it lightly. "I've been worried about you."

"I'm fine." Cassy managed to speak. "I've been worried about you. You look like you've been pretty beat up."

"I feel like I've been pretty beat up. I'm going to be fine though. I got a chance to call Gus Thompson and he's going to make sure the farm's taken care of until we get out of this place so don't worry about anything. You just concentrate on getting better."

"What about you?" Cassy asked. "How do you plan on taking care of the cattle and running around the farm with a cast on your leg?"

"You don't know me very well, do you? I can manage just about anything. You wait and see."

Cassy knew he was just trying to make her not worry about how the ranch was going to be taken care of, but she was worried. Colt was always there to take care of things when her grandfather was sick. Now there wasn't anyone she knew of to help for a long period of time.

"I know you don't believe me Cassy, but everything will be fine. You get better and let me worry about the farm. It's been my responsibility for a long time now. I can handle it."

Cassy could see he was serious. She felt better, but was still worried. She didn't know how, but she believed he could do what he said. She closed her eyes and fell back to sleep.

CHAPTER TWENTYEIGHT

Colt sat by Cassy's bedside for a while after she fell asleep. He didn't want to leave her alone. He knew he was lucky she was still here with him and he didn't want to let her out of his sight.

"Mr. Matthews." Colt turned to see Detective Sloan and Rogers standing outside Cassy room. "May we talk to you?"

"Sure." Colt managed to turn his wheelchair around to face the two detectives. "What can I do for you?"

"We wanted to ask you some questions about the accident. Do you feel up to answering?" Detective Sloan asked.

"I'm fine. I don't know what I can tell you, but ask away." Colt placed his hands in his lap as he waited for them to ask away.

"Can you remember what happened to make you roll your truck?" Detective Sloan asked.

"I just remember trying to brake to slow down because there was another truck topping the hill and there was nothing."

"What do you mean there was nothing." Detective Sloan asked.

"I mean I could put the brake pedal all the way to the floor and there was nothing. The truck wouldn't slow down at all. There were no brakes." Colt didn't want to think about it for very long. He turned around to look at Cassy just to make sure she was still there asleep.

"What did you do then?" Detective Rogers asked.

"I tried to run into the piles of gravel to give us some traction and slow us down. I looked for something to run into besides the ditch to slow us down. I couldn't find anything. The next thing I knew there was a dump truck coming over the hill and I tried to move over the best I could and I must've gone too far. I was in the ditch and we rolled." Colt rubbed his head. "I don't know how the brakes could've gone that fast. I just had the truck in for service last week and she checked out perfect."

"We don't believe this was an accident, Mr. Matthews. With everything Ms. Conner told us about her grandfather, the recording she provided us and now this. We believe they may all be connected. We would like your permission to inspect your truck." Detective Sloan asked.

"Sure, whatever you need." Colt couldn't believe what he was hearing. "So, you think someone did this to try and hurt us? Cassy and me?"

"We aren't sure Mr. Matthews, but please, don't mention this to anyone. We need to be able to investigate without it getting out."

"Sure. I won't say a word," Colt replied.

"We would like permission to inspect Ms. Conner truck also. We want to make sure the same thing wasn't done to her truck," Detective Rogers said.

"Go ahead. Inspect whatever you need if it'll prove what you want it to. By the way Detective Sloan, Lucas Harding was at the Conner Ranch last night. He stopped by, I believe, to just be a pest to Cassy. I watched him get in his truck and drive away. Are you thinking he had something to do with this?"

"I really don't want to say yes or no. I know we want to do some more investigating. You and Ms. Conner will be the first to know what we find out."

Colt shook Detective Sloan and Rogers hands as they turned to leave.

"We'll be in touch. If you think of anything you think might help us, please call."

"Thank you for stopping by." Colt let out a huge sigh.

****

"Colt." Cassy woke up looking around the empty hospital room. Everything started coming back. She remembered the look on Colt's face as he tried to control the truck. After that, everything went blank. The next thing she remembered was waking up in the hospital emergency room. Why didn't she put on her seatbelt? She closed her eyes and tried to black out the memories.

Suddenly, a chill ran down her body. She felt there was someone else in the room with her, but it was dark. It must be a nurse. They were coming in at all times of the day and night. Normally the nurses turn on the light above the bed when they entered her room. She began to panic.

Feeling for the call button, she couldn't find it attached to her pillow. She tried to push the button on the handrail on side of the bed or find the button to turn on the lights, but the rails were down. She didn't know why be she was beginning to panic. She could feel her heart beating faster and her breathing getting shallow.

"Who's there?" Cassy asked. "I know someone's in my room. Why don't you tell me who you are?"

"You were sleeping so peacefully, I didn't want to interrupt you."

Cassy recognized the male voice. It was Lucas. What was he doing here in the dark? Cassy wasn't even sure what time of the day or night it was. She wasn't even sure what day it was.

"Lucas, is that you?" Cassy asked.

"Very good, Cassy. I should've known you would recognize my voice even if you couldn't see me. Maybe I shouldn't have said anything."

"What are you doing here? It's late. Why aren't you home in bed?" Cassy was confused.

"I wanted to see you, Sis." Lucas moved closer to her bed. "I was so worried about you and I couldn't sleep. I just wanted to see for myself you were all right."

Cassy felt him sit down on the side of the bed. She could make out his shadow from the light shining through the door he'd left open just a crack.

"I heard about your and Colt's accident and I wanted to see for myself you were all right."

He was a lot closer to her than she felt comfortable with. "We're both going to be fine."

"That's what I hear about Colt, but you hit your head pretty hard. They're watching you pretty close because you've been going in and out of consciousness. You see it wouldn't be uncommon at all for someone who hit their head as hard as you did to just drift off into a coma or stop breathing all together."

Lucas laughed the evil laugh Cassy remembered from the other night when he was at the farm.

"I believe the stop breathing all together is the way it is going to be."

From the shadows, Cassy could make out Lucas holding up a pillow he began putting up to her face.

"It's been nice knowing you, Sis. It's too bad we didn't have more time to get to know each other better. If you would've kept you nose out of my business, it wouldn't come to this."

Cassy put her hands up to stop the pillow from covering her face.

"What are you talking about, your business?" Cassy asked trying to distract him.

"You interfered with my mother. She should've never told you my secret. I knew I couldn't trust her to keep her mouth shut. Even if she's out in space most the time, she remembers everything. Now you're the only other one who knows about me giving your grandfather an extra shot of insulin. Or should I say, our grandfather. I can take care of my mother with a claim that she's crazy, but don't have an explanation for you and what you know. I guess that means I have to take care of you the easy way."

Cassy could feel the pillow begin to cover her face as she tried to push it away. The harder she tried to push it off, the harder Lucas pushed it against her face. It was getting difficult to get a breath. She wanted to scream, but she couldn't get enough air. She tried kicking, but her legs and feet where held tight by the bed sheets. All she could think about was Colt. This time he couldn't save her.

She could feel herself losing ground, then suddenly a heavy weight fell across her on the bed. Lucas's grip on the pillow loosened. She tossed the pillow off her face and began gasping for breath. She looked to see Lucas laying across her on the bed out cold.

"Cassy! Are you all right?"

She couldn't believe her ears. It was Colt. She could feel him trying to drag Lucas off the top of her. "What's going on? Colt? Tell me that's you!" Cassy tried to speak as she gasped for air.

"It's me Cassy. It's me. Just stay still."

Suddenly the lights in the room came on. Cassy could see Colt trying to balance in his wheelchair while he was tugging Lucas's leg to get him off the bed.

Two police officers came running in the room grabbing Lucas as he began to come to. Laying him face down on the floor and locking his hand in handcuffs.

"Are you all right, Ms. Conner?" One of the police officers asked. "The nurse has paged Dr. Jones. She should be here soon."

Colt had managed to work his way up on the bed with Cassy. He held her so close she thought she was going to run out of air again.

"I'm fine, Colt." She patted his arm. "How did you know Lucas was here?"

"I didn't. I couldn't sleep so I rolled down here to check on you. Thank goodness I did."

"Yes, thank goodness you did. He was trying to suffocate me. He told me he gave grandfather the shot of insulin that killed him. He told me he had to get rid of me since his mother told me his secret."

"He was trying to kill you, Cassy. Detective Sloan and Rogers seem to think he was the reason we had the accident. They're checking out my truck to see exactly what caused me to lose my brakes."

"I can't believe any of this. It's like a story out of a murder mystery novel." Cassy held on to Colt as tight as she could. "Stay with me until the doctor gets here?"

"You just try to get rid of me."

They both watched as the two police officers stood Lucas up and walked him out of the room.

"Where are you taking him?" Cassy asked.

"He's going to jail. I'm sure he'll be there for a long time," One of the police officers replied as they tried to keep Lucas on his feet.

Cassy let out a sigh of relief as she held on to Colt.

"Does this mean we can go shopping for that diamond now?" Cassy laughed.

"Yes, it does. That's exactly what it means."

CHAPTER TWENTYNINE

"Good morning ladies."

Cassy turned to see Colt walking in the door way of her hospital room on crutches.

"Look at you, up and mobile."

"Dr. Williams said I could go home. What about Cassy, Dr. Jones? Can she go home with me?" Colt asked.

Cassy's doing very well. Her injuries are healing well, but I'd like to keep her one more night. It's nothing serious, just a precaution."

"I was hoping she could go home with me today, but if you need to keep her. I'd rather be safe than sorry." Colt made his way towards Cassy's bed and sat down on the edge.

"How about if we have that lunch I promised you before I head back to the farm? I called Fannie. She said she would make us one of her delicious cheeseburgers and have it delivered here by lunch."

"That sounds great and that's really sweet of Fannie." Cassy smiled.

"Yes, it is. There's nothing she wouldn't do for me." Colt laughed.

"Not funny Colt!" Cassy exclaimed.

"Well, I'm going to leave to two of you alone. I'll be back to check on you after lunch, Cassy. Enjoy that cheeseburger."

"Thank you, Dr. Jones. I'll see you after lunch." Cassy looked at Colt with disappointment on her face. "I really wanted to go home with you today. I've missed you, Colt."

"I've missed you too. It's only one more night and we'll be back at the ranch together. We won't have to worry about Lucas anymore. He's going away for a long time. We can start planning our wedding."

"I'm a very lucky lady." Cassy pulled Colt close and kissed him. She'd missed that too. She would love to have him climb in bed with her, but her thoughts were interrupted by someone clearing their throat.

They both turned around to see Fannie standing in the doorway.

"Sorry to interrupt, but I have a lunch delivery."

"Fannie, come in." Cassy smiled. "It's good to see you."

"Hi, Fannie." Cassy watched Colt stand up from the bed and kiss her on the cheek. "It means a lot you would bring these over to us. Cassy has been craving one of your cheeseburgers for a while now."

"So, you guys are both doing better, I take it?" Fannie asked.

"Yes. In fact, I get to go home today. Dr. Jones wants to keep Cassy one more night. She'll be able to go home tomorrow."

"I'm glad to hear it." Fannie gave Colt a hug. "I have to get back to the café. Enjoy your burgers."

"Thank you again Fannie. We'll stop by and see you tomorrow when I pick up Cassy and before we leave."

"I'd like that. You've got a good one there, Cassy. Make sure you hold on to him."

"Thank you, Fannie. I plan on it." Cassy smiled as she watched Fannie walk out of the door.

"I can see I have some competition." Cassy rubbed Colt's arm.

"Not at all. There's no one who can compete with you."

Cassy hugged him tightly. She didn't want to let him go, but those cheeseburgers smelled almost as wonderful as he did. "I'm starving. How about buying a girl a cheeseburger?"

"I can do that."

Cassy moved the bed tray closer to the bed so they both could reach them. She opened the container and took a bite. "Oh my, these are wonderful."

"Yes, they are. How about if we serve them at our wedding?" Colt took another bite of his burger.

"Funny." Cassy grinned.

****

"I hope we aren't interrupting."

"No, not at all. Please come in." Cassy waved her hand.

Detective Sloan and Rogers walked in her hospital room door. "May we talk to you two for a minute?"

"Yes, please sit down." Cassy adjusted herself in bed, pulling her blanket up over her.

"I'd stand up and shake your hand, but it's a little difficult these days." Colt laughed.

"Don't worry Colt. You stay put. We have some news to share with you guys." Detective Sloan laughed.

"Is it good news?" Cassy asked.

"I'm not sure if it's good or not. We had your truck inspected and it looks like the brake line had been cut. Your accident wasn't really an accident. It's just as we suspected."

"Wow, so you think Lucas came back to the farm that night and cut the brake line?" Colt asked.

"Yes, and since we were inspecting your truck, we had them check the truck Cassy drives and also Cassy's SUV. It seems the SUV is all right, but the other truck brake line was cut also. We're sure it was Lucas and we know he was trying to hurt both of you."

"That's not a big surprise especially since he tried to kill Cassy here in the hospital," Colt replied.

"Lucas Harding is in jail and the judge refused bail so he'll be there until his trial. If we have anything to do with it, he won't get out for a long time."

"Colt and I appreciate all you two have done. You didn't have to believe me, but you did. He could have killed either one of us and gotten away with it." Cassy shuttered at the thought.

"He's not going to touch either one of us now." Colt took her hand and held on tight.

"I know, thanks to these two detectives." Cassy smiled at the two men standing at the end of her bed.

"We'll leave you two alone. If you need anything or have any questions, please call us." Detective Sloan said.

"We will. Thank you again." Cassy held on to Colt as she watched the two men walk out of the room.

"I guess I need to go home and check on the farm. Are you going to be all right here without me?" Colt asked.

"I'm a little tired after that big cheeseburger. Can you stay with me until I fall asleep?" Cassy held her hand out for Colt to take.

"That's the least I can do."

Cassy moved over to the edge of the bed so Colt could climb in next to her. Falling asleep in his arms was just what she needed.

****

"I appreciate you giving me a ride home, Fannie." Colt replied. "I was trying to figure out how I was going to get them to give me a rental car with a cast on my leg."

"How are you going to get back to the hospital to pick up Cassy with that bum leg?"

"It's my right leg, so I should be able to drive. Cassy SUV is the only one left that's safe to drive and it's an automatic. I'll just drive it."

"You call me if you can't make it. The last thing we need is you having another accident." Fannie's expression turned stern.

Colt remembered that look from his mother when he was in trouble as a little boy.

"Thanks, Fannie. You're a sweetheart."

All Colt had thought about on the way back to the farm was Cassy and how much he wanted her here with him. He understood she needed to stay another night in the hospital, but it didn't make it any easier she was gone. Maybe he would sleep in his old bed in the bunkhouse tonight and he wouldn't miss her so much. *Like that's going to help.*

He knew there were a lot of chores that needed to be done around the farm. He had plenty to keep him busy until she returned.

As they pulled up the driveway of the farm he noticed another SUV with Texas plates parked next to Cassy's.

"Who the heck?" Colt exclaimed.

"Looks like you have some company." Fannie pulled up closer to the house. "You want me to stick around to make sure everything's all right?"

"I'll be fine, Fannie. Thanks for looking out for me."

"You know you can't run very far or fast. Just make sure you get a good hit in with the crutches. That'll teach them a lesson." Fannie laughed.

"Kinda like what I did to Lucas Harding?"

"Yeah, something like that. Heck I have to help you out of the truck anyway, so I'll just stick around a few minutes and make sure everything's good."

Colt laughed as he watched Fannie come around to the passenger side of the truck and help him swing his cast out the door. He got his footing on the gravel driveway and headed toward the house on crutches. As he got closer to the SUV, he noticed there were two women sitting inside.

"Can I help you?" Colt yelled as he came closer to the SUV.

"I hope so." Both women came bouncing out of the SUV barely touching the ground. "We're looking for the Conner farm. We're here to see Cassy Conner."

"You've got the right place, but Cassy's not here right now. Is there something you wanted to see her about? It looks like you drove quite a distance." Colt pointed one of his crutches at the license plate on their car.

"I guess we should introduce ourselves." The little petite blonde replied. "I'm Laura and this is Nancy. We're good friends of Cassy's from Texas. She said we should come visit and since we didn't make it here for her grandfather's funeral, we thought we would surprise her and show up for a few days."

"Sure, Cassy has mentioned the two of you a lot since she has come back. I'm Colt Matthews." He put his hand out just far enough not to lose his balance on his crutches.

"Colt Matthews. You're the farmhand Cassy has told us about." Laura reached out and shook Colt's hand. "It's a pleasure to meet you."

"Me too." Nancy reached over and shook Colt's hand. "So where is Cassy?"

"I'm afraid Cassy is in the hospital." Colt couldn't get the rest of the explanation out before both of the women were on the verge of tears hugging each other.

"Oh my, what happened?" Laura finally composed herself enough to ask.

"I tell you ladies what. It's getting a little tiring to stand on these crutches. How about if we go in the house, I'll get you both something to drink, you can freshen up and I'll tell you the whole story." Colt started walking towards the house.

"That sounds great. We'll just get our suitcases and join you in the house."

"Suitcases?" Colt looked at Fannie.

"You're on your own with this one Stud. I'm leaving." Fannie put her hands up in the air and headed back to her truck. "Make sure you stop in the Café and tell me all about your evening when you come to pick Cassy up tomorrow." Colt watched Fannie laughing all the way to her truck.

"Thanks, Fannie. I thought you were a friend." Colt saw her wave as she backed out of the driveway and headed back into town. He was sure she got a good laugh at his expense. He hobbled into the kitchen and took the pitcher of tea out of the refrigerator then grabbed two glasses from the cabinet and sat them down at the table.

"Iced tea isn't going to cut it." Colt hobbled back to the refrigerator and pulled out a beer and sat down at the table just in time for Laura and Nancy to walk in the back door both dragging a huge suitcase and tote bag. Colt could only hope they weren't planning to stay the rest of the summer.

"So where will we be staying?" Laura asked.

"Well Cassy's room is at the end of the hallway on the right. There's a guest bedroom if you guys want to share the room across the hall. There's also a bathroom close. I would say one of you could stay in Cassy's grandfather room, but he died in there."

"Eww! That's all right. We'll share the guest bedroom," Nancy replied.

"Where do you sleep Colt?" Colt could swear he saw Laura wink at him as she sat down at the table and poured her and Nancy a glass of iced tea.

"I sleep in the bunkhouse out past the barn."

"So, you'll be around to protect us in case we get scared right?" Laura smiled.

"Sure." Colt took a sip of beer thinking how this could be a disaster.

"Tell us how Cassy ended up in the hospital." Laura took a seat at the table with Colt.

"We had a car accident." Colt started to explain.

"Oh, how awful." Laura interrupted. "Was it scary?"

"It was really scary." Colt rolled his eyes at the thought of how he was worried about being bored tonight. "We lost our brakes when we were going into town and I rolled the truck. Cassy was thrown out because she wasn't wearing her seatbelt. My leg was broken, but we are both lucky to be alive."

"That's sounds horrible. Poor Cassy. It's a good thing we're here." Laura nodded at Nancy. "We can help you guys out while you recuperate. It'll be fun taking care of you and Cassy. Can we go with you tomorrow to bring her home? We can surprise her. We didn't tell her we were coming."

"Oh, I'm sure you'll surprise her."

"Please don't tell her, Colt." Nancy pleaded. "It'll be fun to see the look on her face when we show up tomorrow at the hospital."

"Are you ladies hungry? I wasn't planning on fixin' much for dinner, but we can see what there is for sandwiches or I know there's some fried chicken we can have."

"How about if we order a pizza and have it delivered or grab some fast food? That way we don't have to cook." Nancy had a proud look on her face.

Colt almost choked on his beer when he couldn't help but laugh.

"I'm sorry ladies, but you're in the middle of nowhere Oklahoma. We don't have pizza delivery or any fast food restaurants close enough to grab. The closest restaurant we have is the city Café and its several miles down the road in town. I'll show it to you tomorrow when we go into town to pick up Cassy."

"It's going to be a long week."

Colt saw a sigh come from Nancy's lips as she looked at Laura. "Week?"

"We're planning to stay a week if you guys can stand us that long. Besides it looks like the two of you are going to need help that long. Maybe we can help you around the farm feeding the chicken, cows, horses or whatever it is you have on the farm."

"That should be fun. I'll keep it in mind. Let's check out dinner and then we can get you guys settled in." Colt suggested after he took a big swig of his beer.

CHAPTER THIRTY

Colt managed to find something to satisfy everyone's dinner tastes. He watched as Nancy and Laura cleaned up the kitchen and put everything back where it belonged. Cassy would be proud of them. Colt was sure it was going to take more direction, but they both seemed to be able to handle the mess. Maybe a week wasn't going to be as long as he thought if they could handle helping around the house. He knew Cassy wasn't going to be up to cleaning and cooking when she came home tomorrow and he certainly couldn't do much with his leg in a cast.

"So, Colt, why don't you tell us about you and Cassy." Nancy sat down at the table next to him.

"What do you mean?" Colt could tell his face was going to give him away.

"Are the two of you dating, sleeping together, in love, what?" Nancy asked.

"I think I'll leave that for Cassy to answer tomorrow. I'm sure you girls will have a good time catching up on everything that's been going on here lately."

"Really, like what?" Laura leaned against the counters.

"I'm not going to spoil Cassy's fun so ladies, I think I'm going to turn in for the night."

Colt stood up, grabbed his crutches and headed for the backdoor. "Make sure you lock up. I've got a key. I'll see you tomorrow morning bright and early. Good night."

Making his way across the driveway Colt opened the door to the bunkhouse. Walking through the door he tossed his crutches down on the floor and headed for the bedroom. He already missed Cassy. He was ready for her to come home tomorrow even if it meant her girlfriends were sticking around for a week.

****

"Well at least they listened to me about locking the doors." Colt balanced himself on his crutches and pulled his key out of his pocket to let himself in the house. No one was awake yet. It had taken him a little longer to get around today because he had to figure out how to climb in and out of the bathtub with the cast on his leg. If Cassy would've been there, she would've been able to help. As much as he missed her he was afraid they wouldn't have gotten much farther than the bedroom.

He decided to make some coffee and start breakfast before Laura and Nancy woke. He started bacon in a pan on the stove and then ran the water for the coffee pot. He took the bread out of the breadbox and put a few slices in the toaster.

"It smells good in here."

Colt turned to see Laura standing in the doorway minus a few pieces of clothing. He turned back to what he was doing trying not to notice how little she was wearing.

"What do you girls like for breakfast? Can I make you some eggs and toast? Colt asked.

"I normally don't eat much for breakfast. I usually grab something when I get to work."

"We talked about that grabbin' something thing last night. It ain't happening." Colt laughed.

"Oh, right. Do you have any cereal and fruit?" Laura asked.

"That sounds good." Nancy added as she walked through the kitchen door. "Or maybe a bagel."

Colt turned around and leaned up against the kitchen cabinet crossing his arms and feeling the frustration building in the pit of his stomach.

"Ok ladies. Let's get this straight. I'm making bacon, eggs and toast for breakfast. If you want cereal, there may be some in the pantry. You'll have to look. There are some strawberries in the fridge and some peaches in the bowl on the table. Forget the bagel. So, what's it going to be?" Colt waited for a minute and got no reply. Throwing his hand up in the air, he turned back to his bacon cooking on the stove.

"Ok, so you're on your own. One more thing, I'll be leaving for the hospital in one hour so if you want to go with me, be ready."

"Gees."

Colt could feel the daggers piercing his back.

"I'll take two eggs over-easy and a piece of dry toast," Laura replied.

"Me too." Nancy piped in after her.

"You got it ladies. There's just one more thing."

"What now?" Laura asked.

"Go put some clothes on or you're not eating at the same table with me."

Colt kept cooking and never turned around. He knew if he did, he would lose control laughing. These two were the easiest fish he'd ever reeled in. Opposites must attract because there is no way Cassy was ever like the two of them. If she acted like the two of them when they were together, Colt was sure he couldn't take it.

****

With his and Cassy pickup's in the shop being repaired, Colt's only option was to drive Cassy's SUV. It was probably a good idea anyway because Laura and Nancy were tagging along with him. That is if they ever finished primping they were tagging along.

Getting anxious, Colt honked the horn hoping to get results. Nothing.

"Ladies, this taxi leaves in five minutes." Colt yelled out the window. Reaching down he turned on the radio and Cassy's favorite song was on. "I hope this isn't a sign."

"We're ready to go."

Colt watched Nancy climb in the passenger seat of the SUV.

"Laura's right behind me."

"It's about time. Do you ladies always take this long to get around?" Colt laughed.

"We hurried, if you must know." Laura snipped as she climbed in the back seat. "I went easy on the makeup and didn't do much with my hair. I hope Cassy doesn't mind us showing up like this."

"I feel sorry for whoever marries you guys. He's going to be spending half his time waiting on you to primp."

"Maybe, but look at the two of us, we're worth the wait." Colt caught a glimpse of Laura posing in the back seat.

"All I know is Cassy can get around in less than five minutes and look beautiful. I don't think I've ever seen her take more than thirty minutes. You guys take forever." Colt shook his head.

"Can we change the subject please?" Nancy snapped. "I can tell right now I'm going to have to play peacekeeper between you two. I hope you can behave when we get around Cassy. She doesn't need to come home to the two of you bickering."

"How about if we call a truce, Laura?" Colt asked.

"Well, all right."

Colt reached back and shook Laura's hand she extended as a peace offering.

"Great, now let's go pick up Cassy. I can't wait to see her. It's been a long time."

"That sounds like love to me." Laura giggled.

"She'll be happy to see both of you. I'm sure there is not a bigger surprise I could give her. Now, buckle up and let's go."

Colt headed out the driveway. Hoping for a quiet ride into town, Colt didn't get his wish. Every song on the radio was one of Nancy or Laura' favorite. Cassy SUV became a karaoke bar for the ride.

****

Pulling into the parking lot of the hospital, Colt opened the door and climb out grabbing his crutches from between the seats.

"Let's go ladies." Colt shut the door and waited for the two of them to straighten their hair in the rearview mirror, both of them put on fresh lipstick and then climb out of the SUV straightening their clothes. "Lord, help me. These two primp enough for the rest of the world." He locked the doors of the SUV and headed towards the hospital doors.

"Colt, wait up." Nancy asked.

"Yeah, we need to get Cassy's suitcase out of the back. Unlock the doors."

Colt reached in his pocket and pushed the lock button on the key. He watched as Laura opened the hatch door and pulled out a small suitcase. He was so anxious to see Cassy he'd forgotten to bring her anything to wear home from the hospital. The clothes she was brought in wearing had to be thrown out. They were covered with blood and stains.

"Thank you for remembering to pack her some clean clothes. I completely forgot," Colt replied.

"What do you think we were doing all the time you thought we were primping? Gawd, you think we were only putting on makeup and fixing our hair?"

"Well, I guess you put me in my place. I'm sorry. Now can we go get Cassy?"

"Let's go." Laura took one of Colt's arms and Nancy took the other as he hobbled in the hospital door on crutches.

"You're not so bad after all." Laura winked.

****

"Her rooms right down here." Colt pointed down the hallway.

"You go in first. We want to surprise her." Laura said. "If that's all right with you, Colt?"

"It's perfectly fine with me. Hang on to the suitcase and I'll let you know when to come in." Colt peeked inside the door smiling at the sight of Cassy sleeping. He quietly walked to the edge of the bed and kissed her lightly on the cheek. "Hi gorgeous."

"Colt." Cassy sat up in the bed and hugged his neck as tight as she could. "I've missed you so much."

"I missed you too." Colt sat down on the bed. "Has Dr. Jones said you can go home yet?"

"She's supposed to be in any minute now. I'm so ready to go home. I can't stand being in this hospital room without you." Cassy looked around the room. "Wait a minute. Colt did you forget to bring me something to wear home?"

"Well."

"Colt, I don't see a suitcase or even an overnight bag. You forgot, didn't you?" Cassy sighed.

"Nope. I didn't forget. I just had some help carrying it in. Ladies, come on in."

"Oh, my goodness, Laura. Nancy. What are you guys doing here?" Cassy squealed.

"We've missed you and we're so sorry we didn't make it for your grandfather's funeral so we decided to surprise you and come for a visit." Laura explained.

"Come give me a hug?" Cassy held her arms out and they both rushed towards her.

"It's so good to see you both. I can't believe you're here. When did you get here?"

"We got here yesterday afternoon," Laura replied.

"Where did you stay last night?" Cassy asked.

"Colt was kind enough to let us sleep in the guest bedroom of your farm." Nancy smiled at Colt.

"He did?" Cassy looked at Colt. He was smiling that crooked little smile she loved so much. "How sweet of him and just where did you sleep? May I ask?"

"I slept in my bed in the bunkhouse. Where else would I have slept?" Colt shrugged his shoulders.

"What is it with the two of you? We tried to get it out of Colt last night and he said you would fill us in on everything, even why and how you ended up in the hospital. Start talking girl." Laura said.

"There's so much to tell." Cassy was interrupted by Dr. Jones walking through the door.

"Dr. Jones."

"Cassy. How are you feeling?" Dr. Jones nodded at everyone in the room.

"I'm feeling great. Can I go home?"

"Well, let me check you out and we'll see. It looks like you are having a party in here." Dr. Jones smiled as she looked around the room.

"Dr. Jones, these are my friends from Texas, Laura and Nancy. They came to see me, but they had no idea I was in the hospital."

"Well they have an interesting story for you to tell them, don't they? If the rest of you will excuse us, I'd like to check Cassy over. If she wants to go home she better have some good results."

"We'll wait outside in the hallway."

Cassy watched Laura take Nancy by the arm and walk out the door. "Colt, are you coming?"

"I'd like him to stay ladies." Dr. Jones said as she started checking Cassy's pulse and blood pressure.

"If I let her go home today, I want you to promise me you won't let her do too much. She needs to rest and not do anything to overexert herself at all. Do I make myself clear?"

"What about sex?" Colt asked.

"Colt!" Cassy exclaimed.

"It's a perfectly legitimate question, Cassy. I would rather you wait a few days to make sure you're completely back to normal. It's not uncommon for people to pass out during sex with a head injury. I just want you to know the side effects."

"I promise I'll take care of her, Dr. Jones. Besides with Laura and Nancy hanging around it's not like there's going to be much happening anyway." Colt smiled.

"Can we change the subject please?" Cassy asked.

"You can go home. You're doing great. I'll sign your paperwork and I'll expect to see you in my office next week. Call and make an appointment sometime in the next few days."

"Thank you, Dr. Jones." Cassy watched as she walked out the door and Laura and Nancy walked back in and climb up on her bed.

"Okay, while you change, tell us all about you and Colt and how you ended up in this place." Laura asked.

"Excuse me ladies, but I'm going to go get a cup of coffee and see if there's anything I can do to hurry up the paperwork." Colt kissed Cassy and headed out the door.

"That guy loves you like crazy," Nancy said.

"I know," Cassy replied. "I'm a lucky lady."

****

They walked out of the hospital doors and Cassy looked around for Colt's truck. She remembered it was in the shop being repaired.

"Colt, what car did you drive to pick me up?" She asked.

"I drove your SUV. It's the only automobile that works at the farm."

"Did you check out the license plate before you drove off?" Cassy covered her mouth trying not to let him see her laugh.

"No, but what about it's so funny." Colt asked.

Cassy pointed to the license plate frame she had put on her car the first day she arrived at the farm "Cowboy Butts Drive Me Nuts!"

"You mean to tell me I've been driving around town with that thing on the back of the car?"

"Yes, you have. But that one's mine. I'll have to get you one of your own for Christmas."

"Very funny. Where's a screwdriver?"

"Oh, leave it." Cassy laughed. "You won't be driving my car for long. Your truck will be fixed before you know it."

"What about my manhood? That won't be fixed for a long time. I can't have any of my friends see me driving with that on the back of my car."

"Then I'll drive. Hand over the keys." She held out her hand as Colt tossed the keys to her. "Now your manhood will stay intact."

Cassy, Nancy and Laura stood back and watched Colt put Cassy's tote bag and his crutches in the back of the car. Looking at each other they smiled and all three whistled.

"What the heck?"

The look on Colt's face was priceless as all three women couldn't help but laugh.

"It's those Cowboy butts." Cassy exclaimed. "They drive us nuts."

"Not funny ladies. Get in the car and let's go home. Otherwise I'm leaving you here."

Cassy climbed in the driver's side of the car and started the engine. Waiting for Nancy and Laura to climb in the back seat, she waited for Colt to slide in the passenger side then she patted him on the arm.

"It's going to be a long week." Colt put his hand on hers.

"You'll love it. We can all have breakfast, lunch and dinner together. We can work around the farm and help you out on anything you need us to. Twenty-four hours for the next seven days. You'll love it."

"Just shoot me now." Cassy watched Colt sink down in his seat as she couldn't help but laughed.

"Just remember I love you," Cassy replied as she backed out of the hospital parking lot. "How about if we stop and get something to eat at the Café before we head back to the ranch? Are ya'll hungry?" Cassy asked looking in the rearview mirror at Nancy and Laura in the backseat.

"Sure. Colt told us about the Café here in town. We would love to try it," Nancy said.

"Ok. We'll stop there first. You guys are going to love Fannie and she's going to love you too." Cassy laughed.

"Oh, they've already met. It'll be a treat for her to see them again." Colt rolled his eyes.

CHAPTER THIRTYONE

"Okay ladies. this is the Café." Colt pointed towards the building in front of them. "Why don't you ladies go ahead and order. Cassy and I will join you in a few minutes. We have an errand we need to run."

"What's this about?" Laura huffed. "You're dumping us at the Café."

"We're not dumping you." Colt explained. "We'll be right there. You guys entertain yourselves for a few minutes and we'll be right back."

Waiting until they both were out of the car and heading for the café, Cassy caught a smile on Colt's face.

"Okay, let's go." Colt climbed out of the passenger side of the car and headed for the back to get his crutches.

"Where are we going?" Cassy watched him balance on his crutches as he closed the back hatch.

"Come on. I'll show you."

Cassy followed close behind as he led her down the street a few blocks until they came to the local jewelry store.

"Here we are." Opening the door while balancing on his crutches, Colt waited for Cassy to walk through the door. "Let's find a diamond for that finger."

"Colt, are you sure?"

"I've never been surer of anything in my life." Colt pulled her to him and kissed her. "I love you Cassy Conner. I'm only gonna ask one more time. Will you marry me?"

"Yes, I will. I love you too, Colt Matthews."

Cassy began looking through the display cases trying to find what she thought would be the perfect ring. She felt Colt watching her as she inspected each one. She knew he was watching to see if there was any sign of something she liked.

"Are you two finding anything you would like to look at?" The clerk asked.

"You have so many." Cassy didn't look up. She continued scanning the selection.

"I would guess you two are looking for an engagement ring."

"You would be correct." Colt answered. "We want to see something you can't miss from a block away."

"Maybe not that big." Cassy laughed. "For a half a block away."

"I think I have the perfect rings. Follow me." The clerk led them around the corner of the display case as she pulled out a tray of diamond solitaires. "These are our most popular styles. Whether you want white gold, platinum or yellow gold would be the only decision."

The two-carat princess cut diamond caught both their eyes.

"I like that one." Colt pointed to the ring in the case.

"I was just thinking the same thing." Cassy smiled.

"Here, let's try it on." The clerk handed the ring to Cassy and watched her put in on her finger. "It's lovely."

"Yes, it is." Cassy held her hand up moving it side to side watching the sun catch glimpses in the diamond. "It's beautiful."

"We'll take this one." Colt kissed her on the hand. "It's perfect."

"It looks like it fits perfectly." The clerk took Cassy hand to inspect the fit.

"Yes, it fits perfectly. Like it's meant to be mine."

"It's yours. Wrap it up." Colt handed the clerk his card.

"Are you sure you want me to wrap it or do you want to wear it?" The clerk smiled at Cassy."

Cassy smiled at the Colt not saying a word. She didn't have to. Her eyes said it all.

"She'll wear it." Colt smiled.

****

Heading back down the street to the Café, Cassy couldn't keep her eyes off the ring. It was absolutely beautiful.

"It's about time." Laura ran up and met them as they walked through the door. "Where have to two of you been?"

Cassy didn't say a word she just held up her hand.

"What?" Nancy came bouncing up behind Laura. "Does this mean?"

"Yes. Colt and I are getting married." Cassy could feel her heart beating fast at the thought of marriage, but she wasn't afraid. Colt was her rock.

"What's this I hear? You're getting hitched." Fannie walked up behind Colt. "I thought you and I were goin' to get hitched someday."

"Fannie, I'm sorry you had to find out this way. I just knew I couldn't measure up to what you needed. I would only disappoint you." Colt smiled and put his arm around her.

"I'm heartbroken." Fannie laughed. "Congratulations, you two. You make a perfect couple. Now how about something to eat? It's on me."

"Thanks Fannie. I just spent my life savings on a ring."

"Colt." Cassy hit him lightly on the arm.

"I'm kidding. Let's go sit down and order before she changes her mind." Colt winked at Cassy.

"I already know what I want, one of your delicious cheeseburgers," Cassy replied.

"Make that two." Colt held a finger in the air.

"You got it. Have a seat and I'll bring 'em out to you along with a pop."

"Thanks Fannie." Colt took Cassy by the hand and headed for the booth where Laura and Nancy were sitting.

"When are you guys planning to getting married?" Nancy asked.

"We haven't thought that far ahead." Cassy answered.

"We're coming back for the ceremony so make sure we get an invitation." Laura insisted. "It's not every day you get to attend a wedding where there's going to be a room full of cowboys dressed up in their skin-tight wranglers. Wow, imagine all the cowboy butts in that room." Laura and Nancy laughed.

"We're for sure coming back for that." Nancy clapped her hands together.

"How about if you guys are my maid of honor and bridesmaid?" Cassy asked.

"We would love to. That would be so much fun." Laura giggled.

"We would love to." Nancy smiled and clapped her hands together.

"Great. We'll find you some good-looking cowboys to walk down the aisle with. It'll be great." Cassy looked at Colt smiling her *you'll help me* smile.

"Yeah, it will be great." Colt whispered under his breath.

"What?" Cassy asked. "Did you say something?

"No. I didn't say anything. I was just thinking how lucky my friends are going to be." Colt put his arms around Cassy. "Almost as lucky as I am."

CHAPTER THIRTYTWO

"It's going to be a beautiful day, Cassy."

"Yes, it is." Cassy smiled as Laura and Nancy walked up behind her. "I can't believe I'm getting married today."

"I can't believe you're the first of us getting married." Laura smiled.

"Why?" Cassy's expression turned to one of surprise.

"For some reason I always thought Nancy would be the first to walk down the aisle. She was always the one to have a steady boyfriend or could find a boyfriend whenever she wanted to." Laura explained.

"Well, you're wrong Laura," Nancy replied. "Cassy is surely beating me down the aisle, but maybe not for long."

"What do you mean, Nancy?" Laura asked.

"Yeah, exactly what do you mean? Are you keeping a secret from us?" Cassy moved closer to Nancy so she could hear what she had to say.

"Craig and I've gotten pretty close." Nancy smiled and twisted her foot.

"You mean Colt's friend Craig?" Cassy asked.

"Yes. We kept in touch after we met the last time I was here."

"I noticed you guys were getting pretty friendly at the party," Laura replied.

"Now that you mention it, you two were gone for a little while during the party." Cassy squinted her eyes. "It's all making sense. You two snuck out to be alone for a while."

"You weren't supposed to know. We didn't want to take any of the attention off of you and Colt."

"So, is it serious?" Laura asked. "Why didn't you ever mention it to me after we got home?"

"Because Craig wants me to move in with him on his farm. He loves me and I love him."

"Congratulations Nancy." Laura hugged her. "That's great. I know you'll be happy. You told him he could move in with you right?"

"He has a farm Laura. He can't just pick up and move. Besides, I couldn't ask him to sell his farm for me. I can move my job anywhere." Nancy explained.

"You mean you're actually going to give up your customers to move here and start all over?"

"I don't have to give up my customers. My web design business can be done from anywhere. If I have to travel back to Texas every now then, I can write it off as a business expense." Nancy shrugged her shoulders.

"Wow, you've really thought this through, haven't you?" Laura looked surprised.

"Craig and I've discussed it a lot over the last few months. I wanted to tell you guys so many times, but I wanted Cassy to be the center of attention. I was hoping to wait until after the wedding."

"That's so sweet of you, Nancy, but we want to know everything good that happens to you. We want to share your happiness as much as our own." Cassy hugged her tightly. "I'm happy for you."

"Thanks, Cassy." Nancy turned towards Laura. "I also didn't want to leave you alone in Texas. I was afraid if I moved here with Cassy, you would be upset and alone."

"I'm a grown girl." Laura laughed. "I can take care of myself."

"I know you can. It's just I would miss you." Nancy started to tear up.

"I'd miss you too." Laura hugged the two of them. "I might just have to find me a cowboy and move here with the two of you. Right now, we have a wedding to go to."

****

Everything was beautiful. Cassy was glad she let Colt talk her into an outdoor wedding. There was a perfect spot in the yard to set up tents for the reception and arrange seating for the ceremony. An archway of fresh white roses and matching arrangements waited at the end of the walkway of white carpet which had been placed on the ground for the wedding party to follow. Cassy couldn't have been more pleased with the way the decorations had turned out. She managed to find her wedding dress and the bridesmaid's dresses at a local shop.

"Are you ready to get married?"

Cassy turned to see Colt standing behind her.

"What are you doing here? You know it's bad luck for the groom to see the bride on their wedding day."

"You don't believe that bullshit, do you?"

"I don't know. I've never been married before, but that's what I've always heard." Cassy watched as Colt moved closer to her. He was so handsome in his tuxedo. She told him he didn't need to wear a tux. She thought a nice suit would do, but she was glad now. He was gorgeous.

"You look beautiful." Colt looked her up and down as he smiled.

"Thank you." Cassy sighed. "You look very handsome."

"Thank you." Colt laughed. "If you're not doing anything for the rest of your life, how about we get married?"

"I would love to. Ahh. What was your name again?"

"Colt. Colt Matthews was my name and will be yours before long."

"Cassy Matthews. Hum, that has a nice ring to it. I think I can get used to it."

"What about Mrs. Colt Matthews? That has an even nicer ring."

"Yes, it does but..." Cassy paused.

"But what?"

"Can I keep my first name? Both of us named Colt might be a little confusing."

"Very funny," Colt replied. "You know what I meant."

"Sure. How about if we get married now?" Cassy hugged him tightly.

"Would you two break it up? Colt they're ready for you." Craig pointed towards the crowd of people.

Cassy watched him head out the door with his best man Craig. Before he reached the door way he turned back around. "I'll be waiting for you at the end of the aisle."

Cassy could feel her heart warm. "I'll be there."

****

Cassy listened as the music played and signaled her down the aisle. Taking a deep breath, she started walking along the white cloth lying on top of the grass. She felt as if her life was just beginning.

This was the happiest day of her life even though tears formed in her eyes as she walked to a row of empty chairs decorated with white ribbon and bows. They were lovingly placed there in memory of her Grandmother and Grandfather Conner, her parents, Colt's grandparents and parents.

Colt joined her at the row of chairs as each of them took turns placing a white rose on the chairs. Cassy tried not to look, but she could swear there were tears in Colts eyes also. Taking her arm, Colt walked with her the rest of the way down the aisle, her best friends walking right in front of her.

Colt Matthews was the answer to all of her prayers when she was a little girl. She loved him more than she could even imagine and he loved her too. Life was beautiful and the ceremony was going to be also.

"You were worth waiting for." Colt whispered.

Cassy smiled as Colt took her hand when they reached the end of the aisle.

"I have to be the luckiest man in the world."

Cassy was lost in his eyes. She could hear the words the preacher was saying and the buzz of all the voices coming from the guests, but she could only concentrate on Colt. This was a moment she would remember the rest of her life. It was the moment she read about when she was a little girl.

There was no way anyone could've described the feelings rushing through her body at this moment. The thrill of knowing the man she loved with all her heart and soul felt the same for her.

C. DEANNE ROWE

C. Deanne Rowe was born and raised in southwest Oklahoma. She has also lived in Nebraska, Texas, and California. Iowa has been her home for over thirty years where she lives with her husband, two children and their spouses, five grandchildren, and her hero teacup toy poodle, Allie.

She has always loved writing poetry and short stories and became a published romance author later in life. She has published eight books of her own, three in her *Valley* series, four in her *Cowboy Temptation* series and one non-fiction. As one of the Stiletto Girls with Magnolia 'Maggie' Rivers and Glenna West, she is an author of ten novellas in the *Stiletto Girls* series.

You can find additional information about her other writing on her websites:

www.comfortedfromheaven.com

www.cdeannerowe.com

www.thestilettogirls.com

OTHER BOOK IN THE COWBOY TEMPTATION SERIES:

www.ingramcontent.com/pod-product-compliance
Lightning Source LLC
Chambersburg PA
CBHW071448170626
46811CB00007B/2503